MURDER AT THE LINLEY COVE LIGHTHOUSE

Discover the truth behind the

MURDER
AT THE
LINLEY COVE
LIGHTHOUSE

KEVIN HILLIER

✱ **green**hill

https://greenhillpublishing.com.au/
Murder at the Linley Cove Lighthouse
Hillier, Kevin (author)
ISBN 978-1-923088-46-7
FICTION

Typeset 10.5/16
Editing by Bookmark Edits
Cover Image by Unsplash.com
Cover and book design by Green Hill

This novel is dedicated to all the people
who have been part of my life so far;

Especially. My father; *Robert George Hillier, OBE - BEM Esq.*
He passed away a few days after hearing
I had completed my first draft.

Rest in peace Noddy, 6 August 1934—3 April 2023,
God Bless you xx.

To the work colleagues that have helped
me the most over the years;
Darren, Mike, Mary, Alison, Margaret, Lisa, Bianca, Sara, Emily,
Hannah, Ashleigh, Tina, Gary and Vivian.

To my family and friends who encouraged me;
Paul, Sarah, Stephen, Andrew, Mum, Dad,
Nikki, Carol, Sophie, and Fe.

To all the Pathologists;
who appreciated what I did for them.

An incredibly Special thankyou to;
Elizabeth; my wife and first editor.

My daughters; *Shani and Anna,*
for all their help, advice, and encouragement.

CHAPTER ONE

KEV HAD MADE THE incision from the neck down to the pubis and had started removing the skin from the bones beneath, exposing the patients rib cage. That was when the pathologist, Malloy, hopped back into the autopsy room, still struggling to put on one of his knee-length white rubber boots. Doctor Malloy had come back from his weekday eight-thirty meeting. Before the meeting, Malloy and Kev had conducted a full external examination of the remains from the lighthouse. During that examination, Malloy had instructed Kev to take photographs of any area on the body he thought might be significant, or of interest, to the detective who was coming in later. He asked Kev to take photos of the bruise on the right-side hip, the twisted, obviously, broken arm, the misshapen pelvis, and of course the misshapen head.

At the eight-thirty meeting with the pathologists, all the doctors would decide between them who did the autopsies that day. At today's meeting, Malloy had told the other pathologists of his early morning call-out on Sunday, to perform the initial examination of a person found dead at the foot of the lighthouse, and that he had to have this patient today for continuity. He informed them he had already started work on the patient earlier. He wanted to start at seven, earlier than usual, so he would not keep the attending detective and police officers waiting too long when they arrived later in the day, and also his pre-arranged lunch date today would have a good chance of happening on time, for once.

The Mortuary technical staff had a similar meeting at this time, the senior technician of the day would assign one of the technicians to the pathologists who were going to do the autopsies, for that day. Darren was the Mortuary Manager and he would normally lead these informal meetings, he would tell the technical staff – Bianca, Alison, Mike, Joe, Sully, and Kev – what he wanted them to complete by the end of the day. Apart from Sully, all the technicians were fully qualified and very skilled at what they did. Darren was immensely proud to have such a wonderful team working with him, and he was hoping they'd got another good and caring person when they had taken on Sully recently.

Dr Malloy wanted Kev to assist him for this autopsy. Kev was a very experienced technician, Malloy always felt Kev could read his mind during the time they worked together; Kev would have sample pots or a new scalpel blade already on a handle, before Malloy would ask for them. Also from conversations they'd had previously Malloy knew this technician, was an early riser so the best pick for the early start he wanted.

On the Sunday evening, after Malloy had written up his initial notes for the patient from the lighthouse, the doctor had phoned Darren and had asked if he could have Kev assigned to him in the morning, and whether he would mind if they started early. A quick call to Kev from Darren, and then back to Malloy, assured the doctor that Kev would be there. While Malloy attended the meeting with the other pathologists, Kev had gone to get a coffee and then checked his emails. He did not need to join the other technicians in the tea room for their meeting as he already knew he was going to work with Doctor Malloy for the day.

Kev's work in the Mortuary was varied. As well as doing the photo editing for the department, he took his turn in the office every now and again to conduct general Mortuary administration, which he was not comfortable with doing. This was normally rostered to Kev during the same week that he was on call. The technician on call knew all the new cases and what stage they were at with regards to the identification of the deceased; and they had the information from the Coroner regarding when the autopsy was going to be conducted, or the likely release date would be. So the technician on call was the person best suited to this role for the week.

Kev had covered Darren's Saturday, on-call from late afternoon to around nine on the Sunday morning, it was Darren's anniversary and he had asked Kev to cover so he could surprise his wife and take her out. The Saturday night was quiet for Kev. The security officer on duty for the Mortuary had phoned him just after seven pm saying that Mrs Cains had turned up at the reception again, asking to see her husband before the funeral directors were to collect him on the Monday. Kev agreed, knowing that Mr Cains was not under the Coroner's care anymore. If he had been under the Coroner's care, then

Kev would have needed permission from the Coroner before the relative could view the patient. He told the security officer to ask her to come back in half an hour when he would be ready for her.

Mrs Cains had been in five times over the last two weeks, so she was able to get herself to the Mortuary viewing room area with ease. All the technical staff had met her from time to time over the last couple of weeks and knew that she was struggling with the absence of her husband at home. So they gladly gave her the time she needed with her husband to process her current situation. She would only stay for five minutes or so when she came in, but it was enough for her to see him still there in their care and to let him know what she was up to. After Mrs Cains had left, Kev returned the patient to the fridge bay, locked up the Mortuary, and went home.

Nothing else happened during the evening, but the next morning Kev received a call from the Coroner's conveyancers' team at six-twenty. They told him they were bringing a patient in from the lighthouse, and expected to be at the Mortuary in around half an hour. Kev got out of bed and put on the clothes he had ready for the day. He drank a glass of water before making the short drive from his house to the Mortuary.

Kev parked his car in the covered loading bay area outside the Mortuary. During the week, the security staff would not allow the staff to park there, but as it was the weekend, they would not take any notice. He entered the ten-digit code into the keypad which unlocked this side door. He opened the door and entered another number on a keypad just inside the corridor on the left hand side wall, to disarm the alarm system.

He flicked on the light switch next to the alarm keypad and took the seven or so steps to the end of this reception corridor. There he tapped on the panel of four sets of switches, which turned on all the other lights within the department.

Kev looked down the length of the fridge room and up at the ceiling. After all the lighting tubes had flickered and buzzed their way into life, the department went back to its eerie silence. Kev felt a shiver go down the length of his spine. This was the worst time to be in a Mortuary – on your own, knowing the dead were within the fridge spaces stretching the length of the department. A Mortuary needed live people working, talking, and walking around the place to make it seem like a normal everyday environment to be in. He went to the loo and after washing his hands, he put on a pair of latex gloves and removed a body tray from an empty fridge bay.

Just then, the intercom phone rang, making Kev jump. He looked up at a screen in the middle of the fridge room, which showed an image of the Coroner's conveyancers' transfer team outside by the side door. Kev picked up the intercom phone and told them he would be with them in a second. He then covered the body tray with a white sheet that he'd taken from a store cupboard from the reception area corridor when he had entered. This corridor also had extra storage for body bags and personal protective clothing. Kev made his way back to the door, and held the door open for the conveyancers as they entered with the patient in a body bag on top of a covered stretcher.

"Morning, Kev. Did we wake you?" said Tall Dave.

Short Dave said, "I bet we did!"

There was only a half an inch or so of difference in height

between the two Daves, but it was enough for the technical staff of the Mortuary department to call them Tall Dave and Short Dave when referring to them.

"Yes. Yes, you did wake me. One day I will be awake when you phone, but as you make it a habit of calling in unsociable hours, I doubt it will happen soon. Now, who do we have here?"

Tall Dave replied, "Shall we unload him first? Then we can tell you what we know."

"Yes, that's fine."

Between them they moved the body in the bag from the stretcher to the covered tray on the body trolley. Kev, with a little apprehension, unzipped the bag not knowing what he was about to see. After seeing the patient in the bag he reconciled the death of this person quickly, it was a fellow human being who had died without too much trauma. This was a relief for Kev, he hated it when he saw a deceased that had demised by the hand of another in a brutal way, or by an event that could have been avoided but which had still caused a lot of damage to the person's body. Kev then proceeded to remove all the clothing from the body. He would then normally take the time to list on a pre-printed form all items found in the pockets and anything else that was on the deceased, including neck chains, rings, he would even list any tattoos on the patient. To speed this familiar process along for them all, short Dave had already taken the form from a desk in the fridge room which Kev had seen him do. Short Dave placed the form on a clipboard; as he watched Kev, he recorded what Kev was removing and listed the described items that Kev was voicing out loud for him to hear.

The staff receiving a patient to the Mortuary would use this form to list every detail about the new patient, they would enter the details into the computer system, under the patient's name if confirmed, or the new Coroner's number that the conveyancer had left for them. The conveyancer was also the witness to all items recovered, and would be obliged to signed the form before leaving agreeing that everything had been bagged and or logged correctly. When all were happy, they all confirmed the form sections had been filled in and the items had been recovered and listed correctly.

Short Dave then filled in another section for Kev. He inserted the name they had for the patient and the known address. He completed the section about where the patient had been found, if different to the home address; as in this instance, it was.

After checking the information once more, Kev zipped up the body bag, covered it with the white sheet, and returned the tray to the fridge. Tall Dave then said.

"Hey, Kev, tell Dave what you do. He did not believe me when I told him that you cut them open, he thought it was the Pathologist that did that".

Kev looked at short Dave and said, "Yes, we do all the evisceration for the doctors."

"Don't you worry about cutting into a bit that you're not meant to; you are not the Doctor. How do you know what you are doing?" Tall Dave asked.

"No, not at all. It's all down to our training, Dave. I can remove the organs quicker and better than any pathologist can. The pathologist is the one that conducts the fine dissection of the organs and analyses the samples we take at the autopsy."

"What happens then?" said Short Dave.

"Well, the samples are processed at the Histopathology lab, and they produce the slides that the doctors use to find out about the patient on a cellular level."

Kev's mind wandered for a second. Most times, Liz would come down to the Mortuary late in the afternoon to collect any samples that had been taken on that day, and take them back to her lab area for processing. Kev liked her. He could talk to her. But it was difficult, as every time he saw her, his mouth would dry up and make it difficult for him to get out words that made sense to himself, let alone her.

"What happens then?" Tall Dave asked, bringing Kev back from his thoughts of Liz.

"What, after the doctors have finished?"

"Yes, then."

"Well, then we put the patient back together again. I clean the deceased, return the organs, and then sew them up."

"Anyway, look at the time," Tall Dave said. "Fancy a bacon sandwich, Dave?"

Short Dave nodded at Tall Dave, already tasting the bacon in his mouth. They went over to the sink, removed their gloves, and washed their hands.

Kev removed his gloves and held back until they were done. After washing his hands, he picked up the form with all the patient's details and followed them out and waited for them to drive off. As they left, Kev waved. Then he returned to the office to create the new entry on the computer system for this patient. Once he had done that, he made a call to the on-call personnel of the radiology department to inform them that he had a new patient in the Mortuary, and passed on the details.

They would organise the scans that were needed before the autopsy could take place. Then Kev locked up the department and returned home.

Kev knew Doctor Malloy was jumpy, so he would change the angle of the tree loppers to make them snap shut, and the sound would resonate around the large autopsy room. He did this on purpose every time he collaborated with Malloy. All the pathologists had their set ways and weaknesses at a certain point of an autopsy, and Kev knew them all. Doctor Malloy scowled at Kev after the noise he had made intentionally, then returned to reading the Coroner's notes. He had the notes displayed on his tablet, on top of a stainless steel work bench. It was two feet away from the height-adjustable, down draft autopsy table that his patient was on. The patient was the only one being autopsied this morning in one of the six bays -containing tables, smart boards, and sink areas throughout the room. The lights in the room were intense. There were theatre lights above the tables within the bays, and super-bright ceiling lights around the outskirts of the room. After working in there for a while, with all the reflections from the stainless steel and the noise of the electric bone saws you had a lasting headache.

"I suppose we're expecting the police soon," Doctor Malloy said this without looking towards Kev.

"Yes, Doctor. They are due at nine-thirty."

Malloy turned on his heels towards the deceased and Kev, rubber boots squeaking on the polished concrete floor, and asked, "Are we allowed to start the internal examination before they arrive?"

"Yes, I have checked with the Coroner's office, and they said they were happy for us to start. The police photographer, scene of crime officer, and the investigating detective are coming for answers on this one. It could just be an accident, or a suicide."

"Well, let's find out what the patient has to tell us then, Kev," Malloy said.

By that time, on the electronic white board to the side of the autopsy table, they had displayed the reports from an MRI, a CT scan, and the full skeletal survey that had been carried out by the Radiology department after the patient was booked into the Mortuary the day before. The latter was always conducted as a matter of course before the autopsy process began, as it gave the pathologist the best information about any internal injuries before the doctor started the autopsy.

In time, the display would of course show all the organ weights and any of the doctor's additional notes, which Malloy dictated via a headset. This was all displayed in real time so the pathologist could review it and make any necessary changes before a report was typed up for the coroner. It was much easier to flip back and forth between the different reports and images on the system, than it had been to look through printed reports in the old days. On the bench was a keyboard, protected by a plastic sheet. When they arrived at the bench next to the table that held the patient, the pathologist just needed to log in and then they would have access to all the information they had on the patient up to that point.

CHAPTER TWO

PAUL, A THIRTY-SEVEN-YEAR-OLD, HAD supposedly fallen from the fourth floor of the lighthouse. The broken strut and askew railing were a giveaway to the responding detective, Peter. Peter already had questions in his mind, as this was the same way Paul's grandfather (the original lighthouse keeper) had died thirty years earlier, when Paul and his twin sister Suzie were just seven years old. Peter knew this, as he was a good friend of Paul's and had grown up with him. The first police officer on the scene, said there had been no witnesses to this latest incident.

Paul's father David had been offered the job as lighthouse keeper, the day after his father died, he considered it for a couple of days and then turned it down. Shortly afterwards, the light was automated, and the Lighthouse keeper's job was gone for good. However, when the lighthouse became part of the World Heritage Group years later, Paul had jumped at the chance to become caretaker of the light and its grounds. The Board had received many resumés when they advertised the position of caretaker, but after seeing Paul's application, they decided to offer him the job without seeing the other applicants. His age was against him as he was only twenty at the time. However, his application conveyed an enthusiasm and knowledge of the light and the surrounding area that got him in first spot for the job.

Paul's father was the owner of five working fishing boats and he made a point to only employ local people. It was a way of giving back to the community that had always been there and supportive of him and his extended family over the years. Paul was destined to take command of one of his father's boats, but the lighthouse had too much of a draw for him to turn down the opportunity.

For the last seventeen years, Paul had looked after the heritage site. Whenever he was at the light, he wore the Heritage uniform, which consisted of a set of khaki overalls with the Heritage logo embroidered on the right-side breast pocket and an embroidered image of the lighthouse on the other side. Paul carried out general maintenance and talked to visitors about the lighthouse and the area; he did this with pride and made sure all visitors were well informed of the history of the site. Visitors reported seeing a ghostly figure out of the corner of their eyes on a handful of occasions, but he himself had not seen anything ghostly during his time there. He did not mind if the lighthouse was haunted. In fact, it gave him comfort during the long days as he thought his grandfather was still around in spirit to make sure he looked after the place well.

Paul lived just around the headland in Linley Cove harbour, on a twin-masted ketch called *Seabreeze* that had originally been owned by his grandfather. Paul moved on board to be closer to the lighthouse soon after gaining the position.

According to Heritage records, after the death of Paul's grandfather, the post, and rails on the fourth and top floors of the lighthouse should be replaced every ten years since the light was automated. This was the Heritage way of ensuring the safety of any staff conducting general maintenance or full-on restoration work to the building or the light in the future. From a quick phone call he had made to the Heritage office, Peter had found out they were three years away from the next replacement. This was a sideline investigation for him now, and a low priority according to his Chief Superintendent; he was given up to the end of the post-mortem examination to get the full backing from his superiors to scale the investigation up or down.

For Suzie and the rest of the family, whom he held in high regard, he wanted to make sure that all would be investigated to the highest standard. Suzie and Peter had been lovers a couple of years ago, but his career had ruined that. Peter was a perfectionist in every aspect of his professional life, but he shied away from showing his love and giving his time to Suzie.

"Who found him?" Peter asked.

The officer checked his notes. "Mr Fitzgerald, the fruit and veg man. The local man discovered the body around zero six hundred. Mr Fitzgerald, originally from Ireland, moved to Linley Cove twenty years ago and opened the first fruit and veg wholesale business in the area. A well-liked and respected man, Sir, who regularly walks his dog around the lighthouse before opening his business for the day."

"Where's the body now?"

"Already on its way to the Forensic Mortuary, Sir."

"Who authorised that?" Peter snapped.

"The Super, Sir. He said that he knew you knew the deceased. So if photos had been taken, and everything was logged by the scene of crime techs that attended the scene with the on-call pathologist, then you would not have to see your friend looking like he did. That is why I waited before calling you, Sir."

"Okay, thank you."

"There was still a couple of hundred dollars in his wallet, Sir, so I don't reckon it was a robbery."

Peter thought for a minute and then told the officer to go and inform the family of the death. He wrote the address for him on a back page of his notebook, but before he gave him the page, he asked, "You do have Mr Fitzgerald's official statement, don't you? And he did do the identification for you?"

"Yes, Sir."

"Okay. Make sure all the paperwork is with my secretary Sara by the end of your shift. And make sure that the family know I am the investigating detective, and give them my apologies for not seeing them myself. Tell them how sorry I am for their loss, and that I will see them as soon as I can."

"Yes, Sir. Will that be all?"

Peter nodded and the officer left.

The family and Peter still met up from time to time. Peter and Paul's relationship had been solid before his untimely demise. Whenever Peter got a day off, they spent time together fishing and fixing up *Seabreeze*. Peter was going to do a thorough job for the family. He knew Paul did not normally get to the light before eight-thirty in the morning. So this must have happened yesterday (Saturday evening) or during the early hours of this morning, Peter thought. He needed the post-mortem information; but for now, he would start with a look around here at the lighthouse. Then he would review the initial Scene of Crime report on his office computer, and later he would need to go and look at Paul's yacht, *Seabreeze.*

Linley Cove Harbour was an impressive sight at any time, day, or night, but on a late summers early evening, as it was now, the low sun's rays were enhanced tenfold, reflected by the chrome and brass on all the yacht's upper decks. And the reflection from the tips of the ripples of the water made a beautiful view an amazing sight. On one side of the harbour, you viewed a large, wooded area just beyond the foreshore. On the other side the scenery included the main slipway, the shopping area, and the rooftops of the houses beyond, stretching back for a mile or so up the hill.

Seabreeze was at the end of the first pontoon in the harbour. It was not a good site for a large yacht like her. If you wanted to take her out regularly for a sail, manoeuvring around all the other boats and pontoons would be problematic. She was an old girl who just wanted to be part of the landscape and provide Paul with a place to call home. After the death of Paul's grandmother, his grandfather brought *Seabreeze* and moved on board. At the same time, he gave his house to his son – Paul's father – who up until that point had been renting a house for his young family.

Paul's grandfather moved onto the yacht to be closer to the water and to the other love of his life, the lighthouse; but a few years later he too was dead. His death certificate recorded a possible accidental death, through injuries consistent with a fall from an undetermined height. There was an investigation, but no evidence of foul play was found. To this day the death remained open with the Coroner's office. Paul's dad inherited *Seabreeze* after his father's death, and kept it together well enough to rent to visitors to the area who wanted the full fishing village experience holiday. That helped to fund his fisherman's life. Later, when Paul got the job with Heritage at the lighthouse, he let him live on her for a low rent.

When Peter boarded *Seabreeze,* for the first time, a wave of loss came over him and tears filled his eyes.

"You okay, Sir?" the police photographer, Ken, asked from the pontoon. Peter had called Ken earlier and asked him to meet him there.

The sudden voice made Peter jump. He recovered his composure and replied, "Yes, yes. Sorry, I knew the deceased, and coming here I have just realised that I will not see him again."

"Have you got the key, Sir?"

Peter had worked with Ken on a handful of investigations, and knew he was always in a rush. He wanted to be in and out as soon as possible and he did not like small talk. Peter pulled out of his pocket a pair of black latex gloves and put them on. Then he took out the key that Paul had entrusted him with, and put it in the lock. Before turning the key, he tried the handle just in case. The twin doors to the wheelhouse opened with a familiar creak from the one on the left.

Peter stood there for a second. He could feel the photographer's breath on the back of his neck, and almost snapped at him to back off; but instead he took a deep breath in and scanned this first area slowly.

Without turning, he said, "Ken, can you just stay two paces behind me, and photograph anything I point to?"

Ken rolled his eyes then slowly said, "Yes, Sir."

Peter made his way through the yacht, pointing to the large windows of the wheelhouse, the port holes in the lower deck, a table lamp still on in the corner of the saloon; also, a half-full glass of Jim Beam and an almost empty bottle on the saloon table next to the galley. All the curtains were closed. The glass on the table and the lamp all indicated to Peter that Paul had come back to the boat yesterday evening after being at work for the day. It was Paul's habit to leave the yacht ship-shape and tidy before leaving it, day, or night.

Peter thought for a moment then tilted his head towards the wheelhouse door. "That's it! Nothing more for now. You can go."

"Thank you, Sir. Are you joining us for drinks tonight?"

So that was today's reason for wanting to be in and out, Peter thought. "No, I think I'll stay here for a while."

"Do you want me to wait in the car so I can give you a lift, Sir?"

"No, that's all right. I've got my car."

"Sir, I will see you at the morgue at nine-thirty tomorrow."

"Yes, okay. Don't be late. Thank you, Ken!"

Peter opened the curtains in the wheelhouse and sat on the bench seat. He ran his hand over the varnished wood, remembering when he and Paul had replaced it, and the hundreds of happy times Suzie, Paul and himself had enjoyed on this yacht over the years. Leaning forward and resting his head in his hands, he felt the earlier sadness come back.

About half an hour later, he went back down to the saloon, picked up a glass and poured in water from a bottle on the shelf above the sink. After drinking the contents of the glass, without thinking he turned on the tap to wash it out. After a couple of seconds, the water started to feel warm. He turned off the tap and dried the glass and his hands, then looked in the cupboard under the sink. Now, that was strange, he thought. He would need to get the photographer back to take a picture of this; but not now. If this investigation was going to be scaled up, then he would send the photographer and a Scene of Crime unit back to the lighthouse, and he would instruct them to come to *Seabreeze* after the autopsy if he needed to.

When he opened the cupboard door, he had seen that the valve for the water and the gas were fully open. Paul would never leave *Seabreeze* like this; when leaving the yacht he always turned the water and gas valves off. Anyone who owns a yacht or cabin boat with running water, let alone gas bottles on board, would never leave their valves open when leaving. If a leak occurred, it could seriously damage the craft or blow it out of the water. He took a picture with his phone to record the exact position of the valves. Then he turned the valves off and returned to the wheelhouse.

He drew the curtains, locked the doors, and left. On the way home after spending a couple more hours in the office, he bought two packets of cigarettes and a large bottle of whiskey. Today had been a long and emotional day for him and he was going to have a couple of drinks tonight. Before getting home, he texted a message to Paul's parents and to Suzie. He offered them his condolences and said he would see them at lunchtime tomorrow.

CHAPTER THREE

MONDAY

PETER WOKE AND LOOKED at his watch. Five a.m. He was still sitting in his armchair. He blinked a couple of times, then focused on the whiskey bottle in front of him. Half the contents was gone; one too many, 'he thought,' rubbing his eyes and forehead. Yesterday, at six ten a.m. Peter had received the call informing him that they had found the body of the light-house caretaker, his friend Paul. That had been a horrible day, but he knew today would be worse. As well as attending the autopsy, he was going to see Paul's family.

He sat in the garden for an hour with a strong black coffee, he smoked a couple of cigarettes within that time, he then went inside to have a shower. The water streamed over his face, bathing his sore eyes and head. He stayed under the warm running water for half an hour. After drying himself and brushing his teeth, he walked into the bedroom. The large mirrors on his built-in wardrobe reflected his slightly bulging stomach and muscular arms. He pulled his stomach in, thinking he must get back into the gym. He opened one side of the wardrobe and pulled out one of the six suits he owned; all similar colours, nothing bright, just greys or blacks. He held it up, admiring the sharp pressed lines on the front of the trousers.

Dorothy, the lady next door whom he paid to clean for him, also did his laundry and made sure he had meals. She stored them in the freezer so when he got home, at any time of the day or night, he could have a home-cooked meal. Peter smiled to himself when he opened his underwear drawer. What possessed her to iron his underwear and socks? He did appreciate her, and he would often give her extra money at the end of the week.

Checking his phone on the way down the stairs, he saw a text message from the Chief Superintendent's personal assistant, Fe: '*Make sure you come in and see the Chief after the autopsy, no appointment necessary he has a clear morning.*' Peter placed the phone in his inner jacket pocket, walked to the back door locked it, then he took a deep breath in, picked up his car keys and wallet, exhaled, and left the house.

Half an hour later he pulled up outside the Forensic science building. He was greeted by the Scene of Crime officer Robert, Ken, and someone he had not seen before.
"Peter, let me introduce Eric to you. He is the latest recruit to the Scene of Crime team." They shook hands.
"Nice to meet you, Eric."
"And you, Sir."
"No, please call me Peter. Listen, all of you. I have decided to sit this one out as I knew the deceased. I thought we could

get a drink, and then meet with the pathologist after he has finished. What do you think?"

Ken was nodding. After looking at Ken and then to Eric, Robert said, "Sure, that's sounds good."

Eric was a bit upset; this was going to be his first time seeing an autopsy. He often thought that if he did not get into the Scene of Crime unit of the police force, then he would have gone for a job within a mortuary. He was totally fascinated by the human body and how it worked and what it could endure. On the other hand, he realised that he was slightly happy not to see an autopsy today, as he was sure that he might make a fool of himself in front of his boss, Robert, by passing out or throwing up.

They all signed in and before they made their way to the canteen, Peter approached the receptionist and asked her to pass a message on to the autopsy room for him. The receptionist was happy to oblige and picked up one of the internal phones on her desk straight away.

Kev ripped his gloves off as he took the five paces to the phone on the wall opposite him and answered it.

"Mortuary, Kev speaking. How can I help you?"

"Hi, this is Emily at reception. The police officers are here, but will wait for Doctor Malloy in the canteen. One of them knew the deceased person. They will only come in if you find something unexpected."

"Thank you, Emily. See you later." Kev replaced the receiver and turned to the doctor.

"Doctor Malloy, the Police are here but will wait to see you in the canteen after, if that is okay?"

Doctor Malloy looked at Kev over the top of the small round glasses perched on the end of his nose. "Yes, yes, that's fine. You know I can't stand being stared at when I'm trying to concentrate."

Kev put on a fresh pair of gloves and started removing the liver for Doctor Malloy, who was at that moment just finishing his examination of the heart.

"It's a bit heavy," Kev said, standing in front of the scale situated on top of the bench next to the autopsy table.

The doctor looked up at the display. "Yes – is that 1802 grams?" He placed the heart at the end of Paul's feet, to make room on the dissecting board for the liver.

Kev brought the liver to the table, still in the scale pan. He tilted the pan slightly and the liver slid out onto the board in front of the doctor.

The doctor looked at the organ for a second, then sliced it straight through the middle, separating it into two halves with his long-bladed knife. They both looked.

"Well, that explains the weight then, doctor."

"Yes, quite fatty. That is what happens when you drink too much, Kev. You remember this organ on Friday night. I've seen you in the social club knocking them back."

"Yes, Doctor, I will! Can I remove the rest of the organs now?"

Malloy looked at the rest of the organs still in situ. "Yes, please do, and make sure you take a large sample of the stomach contents for the lab."

"Will do, Doctor."

Half an hour later all the organs were placed in the biohazard bag within the dried-out body cavity. Kev placed the breast plate (the removed rib section) on top of the bag and used the hose attached to the side of the table to wash away the blood that still sat in pools around the dissection board and the patient.

Doctor Malloy wiped clean his knife set and removed the scalpel blade from its handle, as he placed it in a sharp's container he said, "Okay, Kev, let's review what we have so far."

They looked up at the smart board.

"The heart and the liver are over the average weight, Doctor Malloy. The liver 125 grams over, and the heart an impressive 55 grams over. Apart from that, nothing unexpected."

"Okay, Kev, start on the head, and please put the right Coroner's number on the photography scale. We don't want a repeat of that other case," Malloy said with a wry smile. This was Malloy's payback for the noise Kev made with the branch tree loppers used on the ribs earlier.

The incident with the wrong number used on the photography scale was five years ago but Kev had never lived it down. He had been eviscerating two patients for two separate doctors, swapping between the two and trying to keep one step ahead of them. It was an easy mistake to make. Since then the technicians could assist on a couple of autopsies per day if necessary, but would only work on one patient at a time.

Kev always placed a scale in every photo he took for the doctors. As well as showing the measurement of an organ or wound, it had a section where you could write the patient's name; but normally everyone just used the Coroner's assigned number to identify all the photos taken on that autopsy.

"Photos at every stage please, Kev."

"Will do, Doctor."

Kev took the first five shots in quick succession. Front, sides, back, and the top. Then Doctor Malloy parted Paul's hair and held the scale in position so Kev could take a couple of close-up photos of the large gash on the right-side temporal area of the man's head.

"Do autopsies always take this long?" Eric asked the three he was sitting with in general, rather than asking Peter, Ken, or Robert directly.

"They take as long as they take," Robert responded. "We were here for seven hours once. Do you remember that one, Peter?"

"I sure do, Robert."

Eric's stomach was rumbling and he was regretting turning down the bacon sandwich offer from Robert earlier on. He glanced up at the clock. Ten-thirty. Still, if they were here much longer, it would be lunchtime. He looked over at the menu chalk board and scanned the four rows of writing, trying to decide what he would have.

Kev lifted Paul's head with his right hand and with his left picked up a head block which he had put nearby on the table earlier. He placed it under the back of Paul's head to alter the angle of the head and to lift it off the table, so the saw he was going to use to remove part of the skull, could be positioned all the way around the skull without being impeded by the table.

Kev then poured water over the head and parted the hair; he looked up at Malloy. Malloy nodded, and before he could blink, Kev had made the single incision from behind the left ear, up and over the top of the head, and down the other side, ending behind the right ear.

"Careful, Kev. We don't want to dislodge any bone fragments before we get a couple of good photos."

Kev was nodding, but at the same time, with his fingers he peeled the top half of the skin away from the skull, using his scalpel every now and again to cut through any stubborn areas. Once the top section was reflected forward, covering most of Paul's face, he mainly used the scalpel to reflect the bottom half of the scalp down to the base of the skull. Four photos recorded the top, sides and back of the exposed skull.

Doctor Malloy moved around the top end of the table, getting the scale in the right position for the next photo he wanted Kev to take. "And one more, Kev, just here. Nice and tight, please. Now, this is interesting, Kev." Doctor Malloy picked up his scalpel which had a new blade attached that Kev must have put on for him sometime within the last few minutes. He used the very tip of the blade to lift a small circle of broken skull fragments from the middle of the larger oval-shaped fracture.

"Kev, a couple more photos, please." Malloy placed the scale where he wanted the area of the photo to be taken.

Kev zoomed the lens in to the inner section then took three more photos, zooming out a little bit more with each one.

"Can I see them please, Kev?"

Kev turned the camera slightly towards Doctor Malloy, who was leaning in so he could see the image on the small screen on the back of the camera.

"Good, we have it!"

"Can I continue, Doctor?"

"Yes. Continue."

Malloy walked over to the internal phone as Kev picked up his scalpel and cut through the two temporal muscles either side of the skull. All the technical staff did this key step, as when it came to reconstructing the patient, you could use the two halves of the muscle to secure the removed section of the skull back into position. Using a needle with twine attached, the tech would put over-sized stitches into both halves of the muscle (three or four on each side); this meant that when the inside-out skin was folded back and sewn together, the skull cap would not dislodge from its natural position.

"Good morning, Emily. It's doctor Malloy. Would you be a dear and fetch the Detective for my patient and tell him I need to see him in the Mortuary in, let's say, half an hour." He looked towards Kev for approval; Kev was nodding.

"Of course, Doctor Malloy. I will do that for you soon. Goodbye."

As soon as Malloy put the phone down, Kev started up the bone saw and then placed it against the skull. Two minutes later, he was carefully lifting the section of skull away from the dura which lined the brain beneath, using his fingers to release the stubborn areas.

"There is a lot of haemorrhage, Doctor."

"Photos, Kev, please. Two should be sufficient."

Malloy looked over Kev's shoulder at the large mass of congealed black blood, which could be seen under the fine dura membrane. Kev took two more photos just to make sure they got it from every angle. Ten minutes later, the brain had been removed, weighed, and sliced into by Malloy. He then displayed the slices on a different dissecting board so Kev could take photos of the overall view of the whole brain sliced, and then a couple of individual slices that Malloy wanted for part of his eventual report to the detective and the Coroner. Kev then placed the brain sections within a bag and put it at the head end of the table. He washed down the patient and the table. After a few minutes, the down draft of air from the overhead canopy had dried the patient a little, so then he placed a sheet over the deceased, ready for the police team to come into the autopsy room.

Emily was due to go for her morning break within the half hour period when she had taken the call from Doctor Malloy. Her replacement for her half hour break turned up ten minutes later but was now just hanging around chatting to the staff within the reception area. Emily asked her if she could take her break a couple of minutes early, so she could go to the canteen and order her coffee and snack before taking the Detective and the police officers to the Mortuary.

"Course you can, doll," the older receptionist replied. Emily logged out of the computer and wiped over the keyboard with an alcohol wipe before leaving the desk.

Emily entered the canteen and walked up to the counter but on the way scanned the room to see where the officers were seated.

"Hi, Emily, how are you?"

"I'm fine, thank you. Could I please get a cheese and ham toasted sandwich and a small cappuccino, to take away."

"Seven dollars please, and it will be a couple of minutes."

"Oh, that's fine. I'm just going to take the officers over there to the Mortuary then I'll be back."

"Hello," Emily said, approaching the table. Peter turned in his chair to look at her.

"Sorry to disturb you, but Doctor Malloy would like to see you all in the Mortuary. If you would like to follow me, I will take you there."

Eric pinched his own leg under the table and took a deep breath in. '*We are going in,*' he said to himself.

Peter turned to Robert. "That doesn't sound good, does it?"

"No, Peter, it doesn't."

They all got up and followed Emily to the lift. Thirty seconds later Emily said, "I'm going to take you to the gallery. That way you will not have to get dressed up in the protective clothing."

The gallery stretched all the way down the autopsy room along the back wall. It was a raised platform that had a wall between the gallery and the sunken Mortuary on the other side. The wall was around 1.4 metres high on the gallery side. Attached to the wall on the Mortuary side below were the stainless-steel bench, the sink area, and the smart board. If a person of average height was looking over the gallery wall to the Mortuary below, they were protected from the chest down from any contaminants arising from the autopsy room, so it was a safe place to be positioned if you were in normal everyday clothes.

After a short walk down a narrow corridor, Emily stopped and entered a code into the lock in a door.

"Before we go in, Emily," said Peter, "can I just ask if a sheet could be placed over the deceased? I knew him, and I don't think I'm ready."

Emily turned and looked first at Eric and then at Peter. Eric looked the same pale colour as Peter, she noticed. "That is normal practice, Sir. The pathologist would not let you enter and see anything that you are not comfortable seeing." Emily opened the door for them and stood to one side.

They walked past her and up the three steps to the viewing gallery. As they got to the third step, they saw the doctor waving to them from the third autopsy table in from their current position. They approached the table.

"Come in, gentlemen. Sorry to drag you down here but we have come across a possible contributing factor to this young man's death. I did not fancy broadcasting it to the rest of the clientele within the canteen. I hope you don't mind," said Dr Malloy.

Robert asked, "What have you found, doctor?"

Peter and Eric were feeling extremely uncomfortable. Eric had clasped his hands over the top of the ledge to steady himself, as he was feeling a bit lightheaded. He was trying to look around the room and take it all in, but all he kept focusing on was a pool of fresh blood next to Paul's feet, that was not covered by the sheet. Peter could not take his eyes off his friend's outlined body shape upon the table in front of him. The outline he was viewing looked bigger than he recalled his friend being.

"Well, I am sorry to have to inform you," Malloy said, "that we have found a significant injury which has conclusively preceded the fall injury, and I do not believe our patient here could have done it to himself.

Robert could not contain himself. "Murder, Doctor?" he said loudly enough to make Eric jump, and make Peter snap out of his thoughts.

Peter and Eric then heard with the others Malloy say, "I'm sorry to say it, but I think so, yes this was murder."

Malloy then picked up the removed section of the skull and took it to the sink area below the gallery wall. He placed it within the tray. The tray was placed on the side by Kev seconds before hand after he had noticed the doctor was intending to show it to the group.

Pointing with his left hand at an area of the skull to the group, Malloy said, "Look at this area here; this larger damaged area has been sustained as the patient hit the ground. But look here, there is a smaller rounded fracture area within it, and the haemorrhage around this site under the skull suggests that it happened a brief time, possibly a minute or so before this man's fall and subsequent death."

Peter joined in the conversation. "Thank you, Doctor. Do you think we are looking for a hammer-like object? Could that have caused this type of injury? A toolbox was found near the victim but it did not contain a hammer that you would have expected to see in a toolbox."

"Yes, I think that sort of thing would fit the bill perfectly but I would need the offending item in my hand to determine an exact fit to the wound."

"Doctor please, can I just ask how tall your patient is?"

Doctor Malloy looked at Kev, who tapped a couple of the keys on the keypad.

"Six feet, Sir," Kev answered.

"And could you show me the size of any of the person's clothing."

Kev selected an image saved from this person's file "Large," said Kev, looking at the displayed photo of a label from the Heritage uniform the patient had been wearing when he arrived at the Mortuary.

"Just one more thing. Can you tell me if the patient has a missing tooth on the left upper."

"No, Sir. He has not."

"Thank you, Doctor," Peter said, and then he gave a nod in Kev's direction to acknowledge his input. "We will get out of your way, Doctor. Could you send your full report to me by the end of the day?"

"Yes, of course I will," Malloy replied."

"Oh, and I recommend you change the identification of this patient to *Unknown*. The person you have on the table in front of you is not the person we thought it was. I will arrange another identification with a family member tomorrow, to confirm."

Eric's mouth was wide open, and his eyes were as wide as tea plates. '*Wow! This has gone off the charts,*' he thought. He didn't know if he was going to laugh or cry at any second, his emotions were all over the place.

When they were out in the car park, Robert, and Peter both lit cigarettes which they had removed from their packets in unison as they exited the building. They leaned their backs against Peter's unmarked police car, and each took a long draw.

Exhaling, Peter said, "Bloody hell, Robert!"

"It's good that it's not Paul in there," Robert replied.

After two minutes of silence, Peter spoke again. "Eric, in your future when you are involved in this type of investigation do not let anyone remove a body from a crime scene you are attending, until the detective in charge of the case has seen the patient in situ. They have to either confirm who the person is by photo identification, or had a credible witness confirm the identification of the deceased. I could have confirmed today that the person in there is not my old friend Paul, but, due to this mistake, I now need a member of the immediate family to confirm that it is not Paul-so it won't come back and bite us later. Do everything by the book and you will be fine. Okay, I must see the Super now and build a team. So, let us say nine tomorrow for the first briefing in the incident room at the station. We now have an unidentified person possibly murdered by a missing person, and at this stage my prime suspect for this murder is my friend, Paul."

Eric put his hand out and Peter shook it. "Thank you, Sir, um, Peter, sorry. I will, I promise."

Robert and Ken nodded to Peter and then made their way to their own vehicles. Eric followed Robert and got in the passenger side of the small white van. As Peter's car screeched away from the carpark, Robert looked at Eric while he put on his seatbelt.

"I don't think I have ever seen Peter this upset," he said. "Mark my words, boy. From this point on, everyone involved in this case must bring a hundred and ten percent to the table.'

Peter walked into the reception area of the Super's office. Fe looked over the top of her screen and nodded towards the Super's door. People said Fe was the superintendent. She knew everything about every investigation that was going on before the Super did and she disseminated all the instructions to all the teams from the Super. Peter could see her headset was flashing, which meant she was taking a phone call. He gave her a wave and pointed to the frosted glass door in the corner of the room. Fe nodded, and Peter walked up to it, straightened his tie, and knocked.

"Come." Peter opened the door. "Peter, do come in. Sorry to hear about your friend."

"Yes, thank you, Sir. About that – I have just returned from the autopsy."

"How did it go?"

"Not good, I am afraid, Sir. We need to scale up."

"Oh, no! Pick your team and keep me up to date."

"Will do, Sir. At this stage we have an unidentified person at the Mortuary, not Paul. Paul is a missing person, and is now my prime suspect."

"Oh, this is bad! Find out why we thought it was Paul in there," the Super said.

"Yes, I will. Will that be all? I really need to get started on this."

"Yes, thank you."

On the way out, Peter waved to Fe, who held up her hand indicating to him to wait.

When she finished her call she said, "How are you, Peter?"

"I'm good, thank you, Fe. My lighthouse incident has turned out to be murder and has just got a bit more complicated as it is not the person we thought it was, so I will be working on that full time from now on."

"Oh gosh! Well, let me know if you need him to do anything for you."

"He has done enough for now; but yes, I will let you know. Thank you, Fe."

Another call came through, Fe pointed to her head set and waved to him as she answered it, Peter waved back and left.

A couple of minutes later, Peter was in his office on the fifth floor, his office was situated in the far left corner of the incident room. He looked at the roster.

'Okay, who have I got? Ken, the photographer; Robert, from Scene of Crime; and, I suppose, Eric. So who else is available and what skills will I need from the team?' Once he had made his decision, he gave a list of people to his secretary Sara and asked her to contact them all and confirm that they would all be there in the morning for a first briefing on the Linley Cove Lighthouse murder inquiry.

After spending a bit of time sorting things out in the office, Peter told Sara that he was going to see Paul's family.

When he pulled up outside the house, he sat there thinking for a couple of minutes. 'Okay, I've got good and shocking news for them, and I suppose they could be implicated', he thought, but he doubted that. However, he could not rule it out at this stage so he would need to keep an open mind.

Paul's mother, Wendy, opened the door. As soon as she saw Peter she burst into tears. She wrapped her arms around him and squeezed him hard. Tears fell over the back of Peter's jacket.

"It's okay," he said. "Can we go in we need to talk."

She loosened her embrace and took a step back, taking the handkerchief he was holding out for her. "Sorry, Peter," she sobbed.

"Are David and Suzie in?"

Wendy pointed to the garden; she led the way. "David! Suzie! Peter's here."

They had a large open plan garden, around seven hundred

square metres of space. The garden had trees dotted around the main area, and there were borders of native plants around them. The fence borders had trees within them as well. David and Suzie were seated at the end of the garden under a large gazebo. They stood up and headed towards him when they saw him enter the garden.

"Peter!" David said, he embraced him and gave him a couple of pats on his back before releasing him.

David stood back and sat down. Then Suzie was in Peter's arms.

"Now listen, I need to talk to you all. There has been a development which is good in one way but not in another."

David said, "What do you mean?" with a puzzled expression on his face.

"Let me explain – this is going to be a lot to take in."

Wendy began to sob again, clenching the hanky close to her mouth to try to stifle the noise. Both of her hands were clenched tighter than normal around the crumpled-up material.

Peter cleared his throat and positioned himself on the front edge of a wicker garden chair that he had sat in. He explained to them, that he had attended the autopsy earlier. He told them that when he entered the autopsy room, the person he had seen there was covered by a sheet but he could see that the outline was too big to be Paul. By asking a few questions he had confirmed to himself that the deceased person is not Paul, but he would need one of them to confirm that tomorrow for him.

"That's great, wow!" Suzie said.

David and Wendy were trying to comprehend what was just said and did not move from their static positions. "Well, hang on Suzie. Don't get too excited. There is also some bad news. Paul is missing. And in cases like this if a person goes missing around the same time, and from the same area, until it is proven that nothing has happened to them as well, then they become the prime suspect."

Angrily, David said, "No!" getting out of his chair and walking around it, "Peter, have you gone completely mad? You know Paul, probably better than any of us. You know he could not have anything to do with this person's death! And why were we told that it was him they had found at the lighthouse? That place is cursed, I swear to you!"

"All valid points, and I will get to the bottom of this for all our sakes, I promise."

Suzie took her hands away from covering her bowed head and stood up, "I will do it. I'll come to the Mortuary with you."

"Thank you. I will let you know a time and I'll pick you up myself if I can."

Suzie started walking towards the kitchen. "Anyone else for a drink?" she asked, looking towards her parents and Peter. David was the only one that nodded, and Peter shook his head. Wendy didn't answer; her eyes were cast downwards and her head slightly bowed. She was just staring at the slightly moving blades of grass around her feet. David positioned himself behind her chair and rubbed her shoulders.

"It's okay, love. We will find Paul and help him prove that he had nothing to do with this horrible thing!" She remained in her trance-like state.

Suzie returned to the garden with two large glasses of whisky and two glasses of water. David picked up one of the glasses of whisky and knocked it back in one. Peter took a glass of water and sat there holding on to it as if it was a security blanket rather than a drink he needed.

Wendy suddenly stood up. "Peter, how rude of me! I haven't put the lunch on! It won't take long, I promise. You can stay, can't you?"

Peter looked first at David; he gave a nod of approval. Suzie then said, "Yes, please do if you can. I think Mum and Dad will have questions for you soon, when this starts to sink in."

As Suzie was saying that, Wendy was making her way back to the house.

"It's okay," replied Peter. "This is a normal reaction. Of course I will stay."

After sitting in silence for a couple of minutes, they all heard Wendy sobbing again. Suzie got up and excused herself, saying she would help her mother with the lunch.

Peter raised his eyebrows at her and said, "Probably for the best."

When she had gone far enough away from them, David cleared his throat. "Peter!" he said. "What the hell? Why did they tell us that it was Paul?"

"I am sorry, David. We cannot get into that right now. Can you think of anyone who had a problem with Paul? Or more importantly, do you have any ideas about where Paul may have gone if he thought he could be in trouble, or in danger from someone we do not yet know about?"

"Sorry, Peter, no."

"My team will soon fill in all the gaps. We're all meeting tomorrow at nine to start this process off. I have picked the best of the team to find the underlying cause of this, and I will give you information as and when I can."

They sat mostly in silence until lunch was served. No one was particularly hungry, and they all just picked at the chicken salad. The conversation they had during the meal was a bit strained, so after about half an hour, Peter made his excuse to leave.

"Going so soon?" Wendy asked.

"Yes, I have paperwork to sort out. I promise I'll give you as much information as I can, but I suspect it will be a few days before we get anything solid. For now, please contact everyone you know, just in case anyone knows where he is, and let me know if you get any leads."

Suzie walked Peter to the door. "Are you okay?" she said, rubbing his back as they approached the door.

Peter turned to her, hugged her, and nodded. "I'll be in touch soon. Take care."

"I love you."

"Love you too. Phone me whenever."

Peter made his way to the car and waved to Suzie as he pulled away. She waved back and she was still waving when he looked in the rear-view mirror, a hundred metres down the road.

Later in the evening, after leaving the office, he did not recall the journey home; all he was thinking about was Suzie and Paul. The remainder of the whisky from last night was polished off during the evening, and before going to bed, he took the shepherd's pie from the freezer and placed it in the fridge for tomorrow; that is, if he got home and if he felt hungry enough to eat it. This was going to be a full-on investigation and it was going to start in nine hours' time.

CHAPTER FOUR

TUESDAY

KEV ARRIVED AT WORK. As he was walking through the fridge room area, he noticed the Manager's office lights were on, he raised his eyebrows and looked at his watch. *'That is unusual,'* he thought, 'Darren is not normally in at this time.'

He entered the changing room, stripped off and put on a clean set of green scrubs which he had taken from the shelf just inside the room. A couple of minutes later he entered the tea room, where he saw Joe sitting in one of the armchairs, – his chair, – reading the morning paper.

"Hi, Joe! Did you get called out last night?"

"Mmm," Joe replied.

Kev picked up an empty can of Guinness from the end of a three-seater settee and another one from under the table that held the chess set. He buried the cans at the bottom of the bin and put things over the top.

"Joe," he said, "you are going to get the sack if you're not careful! Darren is already in and could have seen those cans. Clean up before we arrive!"

At that moment Sully walked in. "Morning, guys. Joe, I am going to thrash you at chess, I can feel it in my bones." "Mmm," Joe replied.

Joe was the oldest of the technical staff. He never went for any of the promotional opportunities that came up infrequently in this line of work. He had lost his ambition. Since his wife died eight years earlier, his life now consisted of the social club every night and work during the day.

Darren walked into the room as Kev was filling the kettle. "Hi, all. Kev, could I see you in the office?"

Sully let out a couple of *whoop, whoop* noises and started chanting, "Kev's in trouble! Kev's in trouble!"

Joe laughed.

"Yes – now?" said Kev.

"Yes, if you don't mind."

Once in the office, Darren explained that because of the misidentification of a deceased in their care, he had to send a report to the head of the unit. "Now I know this is not of our doing, but I just need a statement signed by you, as the receiving officer. I have taken the liberty of writing one for you. If you could read and sign it (if you agree with what it says) within the hour please. I know you'll need time to digest this document."

Peter arrived at his office. The first brief was going to be in three-quarters of an hour's time, so he wanted to get all his notes in order before the team arrived. Emails were answered and a couple of calls made, one of them to the Mortuary and the other to Suzie telling her he would pick her up at twelve o'clock so they could attend the Mortuary and make sure this person was not her brother, officially. He looked through the glass window into the incident room and saw all the team had gathered. They were going to be his team until this case had been solved. He looked up at the clock, 'Eight fifty-eight. That will do.' He shut down his computer, and, as he walked into the incident room, he clapped his hands together a couple of times. He made his way to the large white board positioned halfway down the room on the left hand side. Everyone stopped talking.

"Okay, everyone. You can all get to know each other over the next few hours, or days. This case has become even more complex. We have an unidentified person in the Mortuary and a missing person that may have been involved in this murder. So, we are going to investigate both for the time being. Ken, Robert, Eric, I need a forensic search of the lighthouse and the yacht today. Steve and Andy, I need a full financial search on our missing person Paul, and his family. Nikki, I need you to be the liaison officer to Paul's family, and when we find out who this other person is, I will need you to deal with that person's family as well. Shani, get on with searching missing person records. Make sure all ports and airports are on the lookout for Paul, and circulate his photo. Check all CCTV cameras in the areas of interest for the last month. Work backwards from the evening of the murder.

By the morning, I need to know the last time Paul was seen. Anna, check Paul and the family's social history from, let us say, three weeks ago to the present time. Also, I want you to correlate all the information as it comes in and keep this board up to date please. You detectives need to build your own teams to help you. Choose your team from the allocated rank-and-file officers in the room with us today. We need answers, people, and quickly. You are all dismissed. See you all tomorrow, and the same time please, nine sharp."

Sully was now removing the creases from the bandage that he had put around the patient's head to cover the injury. They always tried to cover injuries on the patients so it would not be too distressing for the people coming to see them. He had removed the patient from fridge bay 33 (of 88). On his way past the numbered white board on the opposite side of the fridge room, Sully had written in brackets viewing room next to the Coroner's Number, which identified the patient in that corresponding fridge opposite. This was to show anyone why the patient was not in the fridge anymore. Sully checked the identification tag against the number written on the board. Normally the patient's surname would be written on this board, but now that this patient was unidentified, they had rubbed off the name and replaced it with the Coroner's Number. He had carefully transferred the patient on the metal tray from the fridge, using the semi-electric trolley to help him get to the purpose-built movable velvet-covered table in the viewing room.

Kev walked in to make sure all was to his standard. He also checked the identification number, as he was the one going to meet the people coming in, and he had to be sure Sully had got the right patient out.

Sully's mentor was Joe. Joe had started Sully's training with office duties, then had progressed him to doing a few of the incisions on an autopsy that they were assisting with. But most of the time he was allowed to sew a patient up, having now learned the technique. There were occasions when, whilst he was stitching, Kev or Darren would see it in passing and tell him to start it again, even though Joe was sitting there and had not stopped him. Darren and Kev wanted Sully to have their standards, not Joe's. The importance of high-quality reconstruction was one of the ways the technicians could demonstrate to the family or the funeral directors that they had treated the patient with respect and care. Sully was also given time during the day to study advanced anatomy books, ready for the exams he would need to sit before becoming a fully qualified technician. During this induction period, the technician was shown the best way to remove the organs in a timely and professional manner without slicing their own fingers off, or anyone else's for that matter.

Sully and Joe got on from the very first day. Sully had turned up ten minutes early and was being shown around by Darren. When they got to the tea room, Sully, in his over-enthusiastic way, had focused on the chess set in the corner next to the television and shouted out, "Chess! Oh, Wow! I do hope you all play. I am a master. Oh sorry! Morning all, but I love chess!"

Darren introduced him to the other technical staff – Mike, Alison, Bianca, and Kev. After Sully had said hello to them,

Darren then introduced him to Joe and informed him he was the current champion.

Sully went over to Joe and put out his hand for Joe to shake. Joe looked up from his paper and instead of shaking his hand, he nodded and said, "Maybe later if you win a game."

Darren looked at Kev and nodded his head in the direction of Joe. Alison and Bianca observed the look and turned to each other and smiled. Kev knew what Darren was thinking: that was more words they had heard from Joe in the last few months.

Joe and Sully did have a game that lunchtime, and to this day Joe has never shaken Sully's hand. Over the following days it was clear that Sully got on with Joe very well; they were always talking about strategies for their games, the anatomy of the human body, and classic motorbikes. After the first week, Darren asked Joe if he would mind being Sully's mentor and from that day on, Sully absorbed every word that came out of Joe's mouth. As the senior technicians in charge of the Mortuary, Darren and Kev needed to keep a close eye on them. They made sure they checked in with Sully every couple of days, asking him questions to make sure he was being told all the right information by Joe, and to their surprise Joe was doing an excellent job with him.

Peter arrived at David and Wendy's house at eleven fifty five. Suzie was already outside and when she saw him pull up, she made her way down the path to the car.

"Are you okay?" Peter asked as she was getting into the car.

"Yes, I think so. I know you've made sure it isn't Paul that we are going to see, but I keep thinking it will be him soon."

"No, don't think like that, not now."

They arrived at the Mortuary fifteen minutes later than the arranged time. Peter parked in the loading bay area and guided Suzie to the side entrance of the building. When they got to the viewing room waiting area, Peter pressed the intercom call button and talked to Kev, announcing their arrival, and apologised for being late.

"Okay, take a seat. I'll be with you shortly." Kev said.

Kev transferred the phone to Darren's office as all the others were in the autopsy room. They were watching Mike's technique for removing a spinal cord. Kev entered the viewing room from the fridge side of the department. He drew the curtain that covered the door from the inside. On the way out of the room, halfway down on the left-hand side wall, he adjusted the light to make it a bit darker using the dimmer switch next to the door to the waiting area.

Entering the waiting room he said, "Hi, I'm Kev, I just need to make sure you are here to see the person we have under a coroner's number of 321 (C) 105". Peter looked down at a page he had open on his notebook and said "Yes."

Peter and Suzie rose from their seats and started to walk towards him. Kev turned on his heel and led the way back to the viewing room. He opened the door for them and stood to one side.

As they walked past him, he said, "I'll be right here if you need anything."

Peter nodded and said, "We won't be long."

Kev heard Suzie gasp as she walked up to the patient. Looking directly at Peter she said, "No! No, that is not Paul. Can we go now?"

Back in the car, Suzie asked if they could get lunch at the Yacht Club. Peter explained that was not wise, as the view from the restaurant overlooked the first three pontoons and his forensic team would be all over Paul's yacht *Seabreeze* by now, in full sight of everyone. He thought it would be distressing for her. Instead, he suggested going to the Black Dog bar and grill in town. She nodded her approval and fifteen minutes later they were seated in a snug.

Suzie had a large glass of chardonnay, and Peter had a small coffee. The waitress who brought the drinks over said their food would not be long. After a very filling lunch Peter said.

"I can drop you home."

"No, it's okay. I need to get a few things from town. You go." Peter kissed her on the cheek and made his way back to the car.

The incident room was busy. Peter took a second to look at the whiteboard. Anna was doing an excellent job of setting it out in a logical order but there was not a great deal of information written up yet. He went into his office and closed the door on the noise. He spent the rest of the afternoon signing time sheets and other documents his secretary Sara had left for him in his in-tray, he also made his own inquiries about the lighthouse.

After a couple of hours, he managed to confirm a zoom meeting with one of the Heritage Board members, but he had to wait until at least six pm as they were in a closed meeting with their accounting team, and it was supposed to close at seventeen thirty, according to the receptionist. Peter had sent her the link details via email and she promised that as soon as the doors opened, she would get one of them to call him.

The time went quickly and at seventeen fifty the zoom call came through.

"Thank you so much for calling. I wonder if you could give me background on the lighthouse and the uniform the Heritage staff wear?"

"Yes, no problem. The light is very unusual, one of a kind you might say. Originally, it was four storeys high but by the time the light had been up for fifty years, it had to be made taller, as cargo ships reported on several occasions that they couldn't always get a fix on her in some weather conditions. At the time, the State government didn't have enough money to relocate the light, so the decision was made to extend it instead. That is why, on the Linley Cove lighthouse, you have the balcony on the fourth floor, as that was where the light originally was. It was easier to remove the light from the top and then build up the structure from that point. Then they just put the light back on, but now the structure was three storeys taller."

"Thank you. That's very interesting. And about the uniforms the staff wear?"

"Well, all the staff get issued three sets of overalls. Each caretaker will have the Heritage logo on the right breast pocket and then an image of the place where they work, so in Paul's case he would have an image of the lighthouse embroidered on the left chest area. The staff at the castle near you all have the castle image on their left side."

"I see. And do you have a pool of staff that go to any of the sites if you are short-staffed in one area?"

"We do, but their uniforms just have the word *Staff* embroidered rather than a picture. The only other word we embroider on is *Maintenance*, for the maintenance staff."

"Thank you. Could you please send me a list of the names of the general and maintenance staff who work around this state, and their identification photos?"

"I won't be able to get that organised tonight, but I will arrange it first thing in the morning."

"Thank you again for your time. You've been most helpful. Goodbye."

Peter looked towards the clock, '*Just gone six–that will do for today,*' he thought, looking over his desk to make sure there were no other documents that needed his immediate attention. He put his leather satchel over his shoulder, picked up the pile of papers that he had dealt with, and left the office. No one was in the incident room, so he turned off the lights on his way out, leaving the paperwork on Sara's desk.

When he got home, Peter heated up the shepherd's pie and ate it at the breakfast bar. Then, after washing up the container and fork, he had a shower. When he returned downstairs, he poured himself a drink and put the television on, not so much to watch a programme but because he just wanted noise in the room to stop him from over-thinking this mystery.

CHAPTER FIVE

WEDNESDAY

THE NEXT MORNING, PETER walked into the incident room at eight fifty five. The scene was so different from the morning before. Yesterday, when he'd arrived, all the police officers were at one end of the room, a sea of black uniforms, and all the junior detectives in their suits at the other. Today everyone was intermingled. Groups of people were chatting together. It was good to see that they were all getting on. It was always worrying for a senior detective when building a team mixed with rank-and-file officers. Sometimes it worked and sometimes it did not, but this team looked good.

Peter placed his satchel on the floor at the base of the first whiteboard. Another whiteboard had been placed next to it, displaying a number of photos. Peter clapped his hands together two or three times and the room quickly became silent.

"Morning, everyone. Let's start with the Doctor's report from the autopsy. The Doctor found a small head injury that had caused a broken skull. The subsequent haemorrhage would have rendered our victim unconscious within a minute and dead within two minutes if no medical help was given. There were no drugs, or alcohol detected in his system and no other cause of death was found. All the other injuries have been caused as the person hit the ground already dead. And the pathologist has given us a time of death, estimated, between nine and ten pm. Now let's hear from Robert."

Robert stood and cleared his throat, "Morning, everyone. Yesterday Ken, Eric, and a team of eight officers went to the lighthouse. We conducted a thorough search of the light and an area of one hundred yards away from it. Within the lighthouse we found a toolbox which had a wide range of tools but no hammer. We found a small area of blood splatter on the inside wall, about three steps away from the door leading out to the fourth-floor balcony. The railings that were dislodged from the post had not much rust on them, but the post showed signs of rot at the base. Today, we are going back and will extend the search area out towards the cliff top with the hope of finding the hammer, the suspected murder weapon. The search on the yacht produced no other person's fingerprints after we ruled out Paul's family and friends. Eric did find three photographs of gold coins in the bilge. He is going to take them to a specialist today to find out more about the images." Peter interjected that he knew Paul used to collect coins. "Yes, Sir, we did find a collection of coins in the saloon which were stored under the bench seat. All of those are in display books and none look as old and of the same gold colour as the ones pictured in the images found in the bilge."

"Thank you, Robert. Now let's hear from Steve?"

Steve was standing over by the window next to his colleague, Andy. On hearing his name, he made his way to the whiteboard and stood close to Peter. "Well, yesterday we managed to find out that Paul was with one bank. He had two accounts, a savings account with 80,000 dollars in it and an everyday account which had 1,000. We also found out that he owned a safety deposit box in the vault, and my colleague Andy is going to get that opened today."

"Nikki?"

Nikki stood up. "Morning, everyone. I saw Paul's parents yesterday and I have arranged counselling for his Mum, who is not doing well. It's all a bit too much for her currently. I have also spoken with the fruit and veg man who carried out the identification at the scene. He told me that he phoned the police when he came across the body. He said that he didn't get too close, as he knew that you don't do that. He had seen on TV that the people who find dead people always get too close and mess up the crime scene. All he knew was the person looked a similar build to Paul, and when the doctor had retrieved Paul's wallet from the pocket it made sense to him that it really was Paul. He is deeply sorry if he has caused things to be messed up. The attending first officer has never come across Paul before. He was only transferred here two weeks ago, and because the head was a bit messy, he didn't check the photo ID in the wallet against the victim on the ground. He also is sorry for this mix-up and his shadow officer has ordered him to do the ID training again."

"Thank you, Nikki."

"Shani, what have you got?"

"Well, images from CCTV cameras show Paul heading towards the lighthouse on the coastal path at nine fifteen pm, and we saw him leaving the pontoon at eight fifty five pm. Before that, he had entered the sailing club at six fifty two. We have nothing before that yet. Missing persons search has produced nothing so far on either our deceased or Paul."

Peter interjected again, "I had a conversation yesterday evening regarding the uniforms Heritage staff wear. They'll send us a list and photo identifications of all the employees in the State today. So check that, and then get forensics to see if the uniform our victim was wearing has been tampered with in any way, especially the part around the embroidered lighthouse."

"Will do, Sir."

"Anna?"

Anna stayed sitting to address the group. "Hi all, Suzie was the only person within Paul's family who used social media. Suzie is Paul's twin sister and she used Facebook, but very infrequently. She sends or receives birthday wishes and only sometimes reacts to one of her friends' posts."

"Okay. Keep on it, and good job with the boards."

"Thank you, Sir."

Out of the corner of his eye, Peter saw the door open. Looking towards the door, he said, "Morning, Sir."

Everyone stood to attention as the Superintendent entered the room.

"No, sorry, I didn't mean to interrupt. Please continue."

Peter spoke again, "Well, we are done for today. I would just like to say well done everyone – we are making satisfactory progress. Keep it up and see you all tomorrow. Nine o'clock sharp."

The Chief followed Peter to his office.

"Peter, I'm sorry. I'm a bit concerned about this mix-up with the identification. Is it going to be a problem for us later on?"

"No Sir, it will be fine. Nikki has talked to the person who did the identification, and a new officer that has transferred to us recently. He has taken full responsibility; the officer is being given the opportunity to have further training and the civilian is beside himself. I appreciate you trying to save me from seeing my friend that morning, but in future we must make sure the identification is watertight."

"Yes, of course. Sorry again. I'll let you get on."

"Thank you, Sir, I will keep you updated."

Kev was filling out his time sheet when Sully walked into the office.

"Have you seen Joe?"

"Sorry, Sully. Joe is not going to be in today so you will have to put up with me supervising you on my own."

"We can put it off until Joe gets back if you like. I'd be happier if he was with me."

"Don't be like that, Sully. I know I'm not Joe, but I don't bite."

"No, no, it's not that. But to be honest, you do make me a little nervous. Your standards are a lot higher than Joe's so I'm worried I'll mess it up and you won't sign me off so I can progress to eviscerate. If Joe was with us, I would be more relaxed."

"Sully don't worry. Darren and I have been most impressed with what we've seen you doing under Joe's supervision. You have fitted in so well with the team and also, the Doctors have commented that you seem a good fit. This is just a formality. Malloy said he'll come down whenever you have completed the evisceration. So, we have no time pressures at all. All I am signing you off on is to complete an evisceration on your own, without making any dangerous knife movements that could cause injury to you or the doctor with whom you are working.

I know you can do it. Go and have a coffee and a bite to eat. Be confident Sully. Confidence is something that comes in time, but it's an important part of the job. If you've been called out in the middle of the night to assist with a known murder autopsy, one, you need patience as they can go on for hours; and two, you need to be confident and trust your training when you are being judged by the police, the detectives, and of course the doctor you're assisting, in the skill you show during the evisceration."

"Thanks, Kev. I won't be long."

Kev called after him, "Sully, the biggest thing you have to worry about is me beating you at chess at lunchtime!" Kev heard Sully laughing. He smiled to himself and completed the paperwork he was doing.

Sully came back to the office ten minutes later. "I'm ready, Kev."

"Okay, let's start from scratch." Kev picked up his clipboard and transferred the phone to the tea room where the other technicians were. On the way to the changing room, he placed the Mortuary register on the desk in the corner of the tea room.

"I've transferred the phone to this room," he said, looking at Bianca, Alison, and Mike. I'm going in with Sully now. So Alison, would you mind looking after that for me?"

Alison sighed but then said with a smile, "That's fine, Kev. Of course I will."

"Thank you." Kev said and he and Sully turned and headed to the changing room to put on their scrubs.

"Okay, Sully. I just want you to tell me what you are going to do before you do it."

"Well, first, I'm going to check which patient Doctor Malloy is going to autopsy, then I'm going to get the patient from the fridge and transfer them to the table."

"Good. Carry on."

When the patient was safely on the table, they went to put on the personal protective equipment – white Tyvek suits; boots; anti-cut gloves (under a set of Latex gloves) and, lastly, a face shield. Back at the table, Sully put a blade on his scalpel.

Kev was about to write a comment on the sheet of paper attached to his clipboard when he saw Sully walk to the end of the table. He put his pen down.

"I'm checking the two ID tags on the ankle and the wrist. I'm also checking the paperwork again. I am happy I have the right patient. Are you okay for me to start?"

"Carry on. All by the book so far. Well done, Sully."

Sully put two fingers on the patient's throat to find the exact place where the clavicles met at the top of the rib cage. He inserted the blade until he could feel the tip was touching bone.

He slid the blade down the skin, paused a bit when he reached the bottom of the sternum, then continued the incision down to the pubis area, slightly curving it around the navel. He did not see Kev write something on the paper. Sully returned the scalpel to the end of the sternum and pushed it through to the cavity below. Kev saw him lift his head back slightly as a waft of a slightly sweet, sickly smell rose from the open body cavity. After extending the incision down a little, Sully put his right hand in the hole and lifted the skin off the organs beneath so he could continue the incision without the risk of nicking the liver or bowel, which were now becoming visible as the incision got longer.

Sully then started removing the skin away from the rib cage. Kev was watching his technique very carefully. When both sides were reflected down, Sully picked up the short-handled tree loppers. Kev was about to stop him when he put them down. He looked up at Kev and nodded.

"Kev, I've only done this a couple of times, and have made a mess of it. would you mind talking me through?"

"I sure can. So, lift the flap of skin and clamp it, with your right hand to the middle of the sternum to make a pocket. Get the hose and fill the pocket with water. Then, with the scalpel, pierce a hole through the intercostal muscle."

Sully did what Kev had said. "No bubbles," he said, even though Kev was standing right next to him and could see for himself.

"Okay, so what does that tell us?"

Sully replied, "If bubbles rise, it tells us that the patient had a collapsed lung. But the MRI, CT or X-rays would tell us that, wouldn't they?"

"They should do, but we do it anyway just in case. If we instil this in your training, you will do it every time you open a patient. Then it won't matter if the pathologist hasn't got that information to hand. Or if you are doing a high-level murder autopsy and there's no time to have those examinations done beforehand, the pathologist will have faith in you and have respect for your diligence. Also, it creates a talking point for the pathologist to any attending officers while they are waiting for you to remove the rib cage."

Sully nodded and pointed to the other side.

"Yes, always do both sides. Excellent work, Sully."

Once the other side was done, Sully picked up the branch loppers and put them in position on the first rib.

"A bit lower, Sully. Give yourself plenty of room to remove the internal organs without catching the back of your hand on those jagged rib edges."

Sully repositioned the loppers and started crunching through the ribs on both sides. At that point, Kev noticed movement at the far end of the autopsy room. Liz had come down from Histopathology and was getting things from a store cupboard within the Mortuary.

"Sully," he said, "would you mind taking a break for two minutes. Review what you've done so far and think of anything you want to ask me later. I just want a quick chat with Liz, but I don't want you doing anything unsupervised. If you cut yourself on my watch, I will be in big trouble."

"Yes, I could do with a wee anyway. I forgot to go before we came in."

They took off their gloves and face shields. Kev headed to

the other end of the room and Sully left the autopsy room via the internal door to the toilets.

"Hi, Liz," Kev announced before getting to the storeroom so that he wouldn't make her jump.

"Oh, hi Kev! How you doing?"

"Good, thank you." "I am pleased I've seen you, Kev. The team upstairs and I have decided this morning that we will go to the Black Dog this Friday night, and I was wondering if you'd like to come along. There's a cover band playing, and the songs they play are just like the playlist I hear you singing to in the afternoons when you're cleaning."

Kev's face went a shade of red, but he managed to say, "Yes, that would be wonderful!"

"Okay, I'll let you know a time as soon as I have more details."

"Thank you, Liz. I'd better get back to Sully. We're doing a training session."

"How is he doing?"

"Good so far. See you later."

Kev knew this was not a date, but he was incredibly happy that Liz wanted to include him in her after-work activities. When he returned to the table, Sully was there replacing the blade on the scalpel.

"All good, Kev?"

"Yes, exceptionally good. Now let's get on with this."

Sully lifted the first rib a little and slowly dissected the soft tissue on the underside of the sternum. When he'd removed it, he placed it on the patient's shins. He picked up a ladle and removed a quarter of a litre of straw-coloured fluid from each side of the open chest cavity. Then, using his scalpel again, he started trimming the neck skin from the muscle structures beneath.

"Sully, Doctor Malloy likes his organs out in three blocks, so heart and lungs together first, and then I'll call him down. By the time he gets here and has changed, you will be long finished."

Kev was right. By the time Malloy arrived in the room, Sully was washing down the patient and the table. For the next hour, Malloy was doing the fine dissection of the organs Sully had removed. It didn't always take the doctor that long, but he kept telling Sully what he was looking for and was showing Sully and Kev what he was finding. Malloy was good like that with all the technicians. It gave them a better understanding of the organ systems, and in turn, helped them with the advanced anatomy exams they would need to sit.

"Okay, Sully, close and then we'll get lunch and I'll give you that game of chess."

CHAPTER SIX

THURSDAY

PETER WAS STANDING NEXT to the whiteboards reviewing the information written on them as the team were arriving. Seeing he was in the room; they all came in, stopped their conversations, and sat down.

Peter glanced at the clock and then looked around the room. "Morning, everyone. This is our third day on the investigation and six days since Paul, our suspected killer, was last seen. It has been five days since the victim was found dead. So, what have we got? And it needs to be good. Eric, let's start with you."

Eric almost fell off his chair. "Yes, um, yes. Sorry Sir." He stood up but instantly wished he hadn't. Everyone close to him could see his legs and hands were shaking. "Well, I took the photos of the coins to the shop in town called Shiny Things. They deal in medals, coins, and stamps. The proprietor couldn't give me much info, although he did confirm that they looked incredibly old and were probably gold. If it was part of a collection, then the sale value would be in the thousands if not millions. He suggested that I go to see the head of the Cove Coin Club, where Paul and he were members. They usually meet on the second Tuesday of the month, at the Community Centre."

Eric looked at his notes then went on: "I then went to meet with a Mr Pomeroy head of the coin club. I found him at the museum, where he works. He had a good look over the photographs, went into his office, and showed me a newspaper article about a collection of ten gold coins that were stolen fifteen years ago. He's certain that the photos we have do show part of that very collection. Sir, he was extremely interested in where we had got the photos. I didn't say anything to him; I just avoided the question."

"Robert. What have you got for us?"

"We're meeting up with the inshore rescue members today. They will be diving in an area that we've identified as a possible place the hammer could have ended up if it were thrown from the cliff edge. We are also going to do a preliminary search of a couple of caves further down the coast, which could be accessible from the coastal path if you had good knowledge of the area."

"Steve?"

"We had no luck with finding out where the 80,000 came from, as all the money was paid into the account in cash. So, we cannot trace any of it. No activity has been seen on the accounts for the last five days, but we have frozen them just in case. The rest of the family's financials all came up good. Andy got the safety deposit box opened and there was nothing in there."

Andy cleared his throat and spoke, "The Bank Manager told

me that Paul had accessed the vault the day he went missing, but he couldn't say if he had taken anything away with him."

"Shani?"

"Morning, everyone. Forensics have confirmed that the word *Maintenance* has been removed from the overalls our victim was wearing, and the image of the light was slightly different from the three recovered overalls from Paul's yacht. We think we have an ID on our victim. I am going through the CCTV, but I haven't seen him yet." "Okay. Nikki, tell us about our victim."

"Morning. We are sure that the victim was Mr Sam Heartland. He did work for the Heritage Group as a maintenance worker. I came in late last night and contacted his mother, who lives in London. As you can imagine, she was devastated by the news I gave her, but she will be here in a couple of days to carry out a formal identification with me."

"Anna, can you and the team get us everything you can on Mr Heartland by tomorrow, please."

"Will do, Sir."

"And any luck with tracing Paul's phone or laptop?"

"No, Sir. Sorry."

"Excellent work, people." Peter turned to his secretary Sara and said "Sara, could you type this out for me and hand deliver to Fe for attention of the Superintendent, so he is fully up to date with the investigation so far when we have finished please."

He saw her open her laptop and position her hands above the keypad, and he dictated: "Thursday, Day Three briefing. For the Linley Cove lighthouse murder. Paul, our suspect, is still missing. He had a large amount of savings which cannot be accounted for, and the day he went missing (Saturday morning) he accessed a safety deposit box at the bank and possibly removed what was in there. We think he may be in possession of information about the gold coins which could be part of a stolen collection. Scene of Crime is teaming up with Inshore Rescue to extend the search area, trying to find a hammer that we think is the murder weapon. Our victim is, we believe, an employee of the Heritage Group, and his mother will travel here over the next few days from London to carry out a formal identification. "

He paused for a moment, then said, "Now, I am sure you have all realised that we will be working this weekend. At the bottom, Sara, could you please add a line to the Super officially requesting overtime approval. Thank you, everyone! See you all in the morning and, once again, excellent work."

Peter spent the next couple of hours in his office sorting a fresh pile of papers that had been put in the in-tray. At lunch-time he went around to see David and Wendy. David opened the door.

"Hi, Peter. Any news?"

"No, sorry. I have just a couple of questions if you don't mind."

"Not at all, come in."

Wendy was just coming out of the kitchen. "Oh hello, love. Any news?"

"No, sorry, just a couple of questions."

"I've just put the kettle on. Would you like a cup?"

"Yes, thank you. Tea, please."

"Wendy, we'll be in the garage," David announced as he

opened the back door. Peter followed him outside. "So, what's up?" David asked.

"Okay. So, we know Paul went to the bank on Saturday morning and accessed a safety deposit box. Have you any idea what he may have been keeping in there?"

"Probably the same as us. We've all got one. I always instilled the importance of keeping important documents out of the house. Wendy and I keep our wills, insurance documents and our passports in ours. And I presume Paul and Suzie did the same."

"Thank you, the other thing is, Paul had quite a bit of money in a savings account. Would you be able to help us out with where that may have come from?"

"Well, I reckon most, if not all, was from a trust fund that Suzie and Paul had. It was set up by us from money my father left us. They could get access to it when they became twenty. Suzie has probably spent hers by now on shoes; but Paul was good with money so I think he would have saved most of it. He did take all the money out to be able to buy his own yacht that he has been working on, as you know. But I don't know how much he ended up with to put back in the bank. And more than likely he would have been adding to it over the years since."

"Thank you again. I know this must be difficult for you. Now, Paul was last seen heading to the light on Saturday night. Our victim was found Sunday morning. Can you think of any reason Paul would go to the light at night?"

"Perhaps he saw something going on up there. A torch light or something, I don't know. You know you can see the bottom half of the lighthouse from the bow of *Seabreeze*. That's why my dad got that first pontoon."

"I didn't know that. Thank you, David. You have been extremely helpful."

Just then, Wendy appeared at the doorway. "Are you two coming in for this tea? It's getting cold."

"Yes, coming in now love," David replied.

When Peter had finished drinking his tea, he left David and Wendy and headed to the harbour, where he boarded *Seabreeze* and, sure enough, he could see the bottom half of the lighthouse from the bow.

Sully was almost done sewing up the patient. To speed things up, Kev had reconstructed the head for him and had cleaned up the top end of the table and all the instruments.

"Good job, Sully. If you clean the bottom end of the patient and the table, I'll get the fridge tray."

When Kev returned, they slid the patient onto the tray. "I'll put him back in the fridge while you clean the table, but we'll leave the floor until after lunch. I will meet you in the tea room and we can have that game of chess."

When Sully entered the room, Kev had moved the chess board to the larger coffee table in between the two two-seater sofas that were facing each other and was picking at a ham sandwich.

"Let the game begin," Sully announced as he entered the tea room flipping a coin. Kev looked up and called heads before the coin landed on the back of Sully's left hand.

"Heads it is. Make your first move and I will beat you."

They played in silence for the next three-quarters of an hour.

"Well, that's it, Kev. A draw, I think."

"Yes, you're right. Come on, we'd better get the Mortuary cleaned up with the others, otherwise Darren will do his nut."

They cleaned up the rest of the room before heading to the boot rack. In the afternoons they did not wear Tyvek suits over the top of the scrubs, just boots and a pair of gloves for washing down the autopsy room. Every day, the autopsy room was cleaned down from the top of the gallery to the changing areas. A couple of years ago, Malloy had taken a swab from the top of an autopsy table after it was cleaned; then he went to the theatre room of the local hospital and swabbed their operating theatre table. He sent both off for analysis. When the results came back, they found that the autopsy room had no contaminants, but the theatre did. The staff prided themselves on this knowledge and it was reassuring for the doctors. They knew there would be little chance that a sample taken within the autopsy room would become cross-contaminated with a foreign body. Therefore, the technical staff always spent at least half the day cleaning, and spent much of their time with new employees emphasising why cleaning was just as important a skill as eviscerating.

Peter made his way to the lighthouse and parked his car right outside the gated entrance. He looked over at the harbour and confirmed that only the bow of *Seabreeze* could be seen from here and not the whole yacht. Then he walked the few hundred yards to the cliff edge and looked down. He observed a line of police officers walking along the foreshore. Three people in Tyvek suits were also in a line, but following the line of police personnel, about four paces behind them.

Just then, Peter saw one of the officers on the outside edge of the line close to the water stop and raise his hand, and he heard the officer make an unclear sound. He saw everyone stop, and the three in the Tyvek suits went close to the officer who had his hand raised. Peter turned and headed back to the car and returned to the office for the rest of the day.

CHAPTER SEVEN

FRIDAY

"LISTEN UP!," PETER WAITED for silence, "This is what I have from yesterday. I found out that the money in Paul's savings account could mostly be from a trust fund that he could access from the age of twenty. So, Steve and Andy, could you get the bank to confirm that for us, please. Now, I know that the whole family used safety deposit boxes to keep their passports and other important documents in, instead of keeping them in their homes. David, Paul's father, also informed me that you can see the bottom of the light from the bow of the yacht. So, let's go back over the footage from the harbour to see if we have got Paul on the bow of the yacht from around 7pm last Saturday. Eric, have we got any added information on the coins?"

"Yes, Sir. We received the photographs of the whole collection from the previous owner. The photos were taken for insurance reasons when he obtained them. The lab worked through the night, and they have a positive match for our three photographs of the coins. They have mapped the others from the original photos so if we come across the coins or more photos, it will be a quick job to confirm if they are part of the same collection." "Good. Well done. Robert?"

"Morning, all. Well, as you know, we went back to the light yesterday and conducted a thorough search of the foreshore at low tide. We had divers go out a little further. We also had time to look in the first of two caves along that part of the coastline and did not find anything of interest there. We are going back to investigate the second cave today."

Peter interjected, "I was on top of the cliff yesterday and I saw one of the officers raise their hand. What was that about?"

"We were hopeful, but what we thought was a hammer handle turned out to be a part of a bicycle handlebar."

"And Shani, what have you got, please?"

Shani remained seated and reported that her team had not found Sam Heartland on any CCTV cameras but would keep looking. And they would now also try to find Paul on the deck of the boat.

"Nikki?"

"Yes, I am arranging to carry out the identification with our victim's mother on Monday morning. Her flight gets in Sunday afternoon, so I'll make sure she is collected and then I will arrange with the Mortuary for a suitable time to go in."

"Good. Where are you arranging for her to stay?"

"In the Grand, Sir. I have approval and funding to let her stay for up to a week."

"Now, Anna, what have you and your team got on the victim?"

"Morning, everyone. Well, we have him as a thirty-nine-year-old who moved from London. He has been working for the Heritage Group as a maintenance staff member since soon after arriving. But here's the thing – before leaving the UK, he was in the Metropolitan police as an undercover officer. We have a phone registered to him and a bank account, but no social media."

"Bloody Hell! One of our own! A Met officer," said Peter. "Nikki, another late-night call, please. Get hold of your counterpart in London and find out why he left the service if he has. And also find out, if you can, the last case he was working on."

"Will do, Sir."

"Robert, can your team go to his residence? And Steve, will you and Andy find out his financial history. Let's get on. See you all in the morning."

Kev was hosting the morning meeting in the Mortuary. No autopsies were scheduled for today, and Darren was taking leave again.

"Morning, all. We have a rare quiet day so we will make the best of it. Sully, can you be in the office for me, and Joe, you can be his shadow. I'm going to catch up with the photography. Alison, Bianca, Mike, can you clean the body trolleys and the fridge room, please. Oh, and if you need to finish any of your mandatory training, please get it done today. You can all have an hour and a half lunch break, but staggered please. Sort the times out between yourselves. And by the way, I'm leaving at four today as I am going out with the histopathology crowd tonight."

Sully let out a "*Whoop! Whoop!*" noise and started chanting, "Kev's got a girlfriend! Kev's got a girlfriend!" The others in the room all laughed.

"That will do. Come on, let's get on," Kev said.

After lunch, Kev put a couple of specimen pots out on the histopathology shelves and found a note on the shelf for him. Just a folded A4 sheet of paper, with *Kev* written on it. He opened it up and in one section of the four squares of folded paper, it read: *Hi Kev, hope you are still good for tonight. It starts around 7pm. We are planning to get there at six thirty. Hope to see you Liz, xx*. He refolded the paper and placed it in his back pocket and went back to the office.

Robert drove his van to the lighthouse and parked in the car park. Robert, Ken, and Eric all got out and then waited for the three police officers that were assigned to them. They didn't wait long. After only a couple of minutes, a police patrol car pulled up behind them. Robert, Ken, and Eric had arrived wearing their disposable Tyvek suits. When they got out of the van, all three pulled out of the back cargo hold a couple of pairs of gloves each and put them in their pockets. Robert gave them each a torch, and then they each grabbed a handful of evidence bags of varying sizes and put them in one of the many pockets they had about their clothing.

After greeting the officers, Robert gave them each a Tyvek

suit, and they removed their utility belts and put them on straight away, over their uniforms. Robert then gave them a couple of pairs of gloves each, which they placed in their pockets before putting their utility belts back on.

Robert spoke to the whole group, "Come on then, we'd better get on. We have four hours before the tide turns and I don't know how big that second cave is."

All five started the twenty-minute walk down the coastal path to the beach below. It took them an extra ten minutes to reach the furthest cave along the coastline. They had taken a brief look at this cave the day before but had not had enough time to go in too far. This cave went into the cliff a long way; it was not your normal cave caused by coastal erosion.

Robert said, "Okay, everyone, let's make this fast and simple. I'm going to keep an eye on the time, and when I say we go, we go. We'll make a line for as long as we can, but as it gets narrower – if it does – the officers will lead the way. Okay?"

In unison the officers let out a "Yes, Sir!" Eric and Ken gave him a nod.

After they had entered the cave, Ken stopped a couple of metres in. Everyone else stopped as well.

"Oh, sorry, nothing seen," Ken said, "I just need to adjust the camera for the lower light, sorry."

Eric let out an audible breath, "Sorry, I got scared then, this place is so spooky." The cave entrance was huge and from this spot it looked as though it went into the cliff for miles. Eric wondered how the cliff top above them did not just fall into this void below its surface. Eric was standing on the edge of a middle channel of water that was still in the cave even at this low tide time of day. This channel of water must have been at least five metres wide and who knows how deep, it was spellbinding.

"Eric!" Eric jumped. "Come away from that edge! That channel looks deep to me, let's keep going," Robert announced to the group.

From that moment on, Robert kept checking his watch every few minutes as he had become incredibly nervous. After some metres in, they had to form two lines, and the officers took the lead. At the back of the main cave there was an opening to a passageway which they had to climb up to. The police officer at the front turned to Robert, who nodded, and they continued making their way into the passageway. After entering it, they walked for ten minutes up a steep incline. They were in single file now but still had enough room above their heads.

Eighteen minutes in, the officer at the front stopped.

"Sir, I can see light ahead."

"What sort of light?", Robert called out.

"Daylight," he replied.

"We have plenty of time so let's carry on."

A few minutes later, the first officer had reached a metal grate. There was no lock, so he pushed it open and climbed out into an open field.

"We're back at the light," he said to the others behind him.

One after the other they made their way out of the tunnel.

"Well, I'll be damned!", Robert said when he was out of the passageway. "We're only a field away from the light, and probably a hundred metres away from the end of our first search area. Okay, everyone, let's form a line again and head back to the light."

Kev picked up his rucksack from the tea room. "Hey guys, I'm off!"

"You sure are, Kev, I can smell you from here," Sully called out from the changing room. All the others then heard Sully giggling to himself.

"I'll see you all on Monday. Joe, you're on call, aren't you? Give me a shout if you need any help or cover. And clean up before we all arrive on Monday, okay?"

"Mmm," Joe replied.

Kev was home by half past four. He showered, then looked at the clothes he had hanging on the back of his bedroom door. He'd picked them out for tonight the previous day. He opened the wardrobe to see if there was anything else he could wear to the pub without feeling self-conscious. He desperately wanted Liz to see him wearing something different to what he normally wore to work. He wanted to go for a smart casual look. *'No, they will do,'* he thought, he got dressed in the dark green chinos and the blue cotton shirt and headed downstairs.

On the way to the Black Dog, Kev stopped off at the Yacht Club, where he ordered a Jim Beam with Coke and a burger. After mostly finishing his meal, he paid the bill and went to the toilet. When he went to wash his hands, the water hit the bottom of the shallow sink and splashed over the top, wetting the bottom part of his shirt, top of the waist, and the thigh of his trousers. *'Bloody Hell! That's not good,'* he thought.

Another patron using the facilities half smiled and said, "Don't you hate that? It happened to me last week. These places get designer stuff in to make the place look modern, but they're not practical and hardly fit for purpose. The sinks are too shallow and the water pressure too high."

Kev agreed and went over to the hand dryer. "Well, that's not good either," he said. "One, you have to walk across the room to get to the dryer, leaving a trail of water on the floor; and then this nozzle – the bloody thing, you can't move it like you could with the old ones."

The other man was on the way out and said, "Anyway, good luck."

"Thanks," Kev replied. He stood there for a couple of minutes trying to dry his clothing with toilet paper. He looked at his watch and decided he had no time left. '*I will just have to go,*' he thought.

He walked back through the restaurant, scanning the room on his way through. He saw the man who had spoken to him a few minutes ago. He was now pointing Kev out to the person he was with. She turned and looked in his direction and smiled. Kev nodded, lowered his head and, speeding up his pace, left the Yacht Club.

When he arrived at the Black Dog, he checked his watch: six fifty five. He looked down at his trousers. Still a little damp. He took a deep breath in and entered the function room.

Straight away he saw Liz with a group of people. Most he recognised, but others he had not seen before. They were all seated in the far-right corner of the room, on a sweeping corner lounge. Kev made his way over to them.

"Hi everyone, I made it! But I had a little trouble on the way." Looking down, he gestured at the damp patch still evident on his trousers. He heard a couple of them sniggering, but he was looking directly at Liz. Had he blown it?

But Liz was very gracious. "Oh no. Are you okay?" she said.

Going red in the face, Kev replied, "Yes, I am, thank you. Anyway, can I get you a drink?"

"A white wine, please," Liz replied.

"And anyone else?" Kev asked, looking at the rest of the group. Half were shaking their heads and the others said no thank you.

"I'll be back in a minute," he said to Liz.

Kev got the drinks and when he turned from the bar to head back towards the group, he noticed everyone had moved along the corner couch so there was a space for him at the end next to Liz.

"What happened, then?" Liz enquired when he sat down.

"Oh, I went into the Yacht Club on the way here to get a bite to eat and when I was washing my hands before leaving, the water went over the top of the sink and got me."

"Oh, the Yacht Club," Liz replied. "The ladies room sinks are like that as well. I know a lot of girls that have been caught out like you have."

Just then the band started tuning up. With her left hand, Liz picked up her drink from the table in front of her and put her right arm through Kev's left arm. She scrunched up her shoulders and gave him a big smile.

The whole evening went well. They talked in between the songs the band played and they really got on well together.

When the band had played the last song of the set, everyone gave them a standing ovation. Kev and Liz drank the last of their drinks and followed everyone out to the car park. Liz still had her arm through Kev's and when they were outside she gave Kev a hug and a kiss on the cheek.

"Can we do this again?", she said to him, "I've had a great night. How about next Friday?"

"I'm sorry, I'm on call from Friday. But I could do the Friday after."

"It's a date," Liz said. "I'll leave you a note on our shelf."

"Can I get you a taxi, Liz?"

"No, I'm fine thanks. I promised Emily that she could take me home. She's going to borrow some of my clothes for her date tomorrow."

"Okay, as long as you get back safely."

Liz gave Kev another hug and kissed him again on the cheek. "Goodnight, I will see you when I'm looking at your face," she said with a smile, then turned and grabbed Emily's arm and headed off to her car.

Kev took six steps forward and sat down on a low wall. *'Bloody hell!',* he thought to himself, *'I've got a date!'* After he had sat there for nearly ten minutes, he got up and headed home.

CHAPTER EIGHT

SATURDAY

"MORNING, EVERYONE. IT'S JUST us today. All the rank-and-file officers are having the weekend off but there are staff you can call upon if you need extra support. If you do, approach the Duty Sergeant and he will assign someone to you. Okay, Steve and Andy, what have you got for us today?"

"We investigated Sam's finances. He had nothing. A hundred dollars in just one account, no credit cards, no savings account. Basically, he had been living from payday to payday, using nearly all his minimum wage within that two-week period."

"Shani?"

"Yes, Paul was seen on the bow of the yacht at eight fifty pm. It appears he was looking in the direction of the light. We have also seen Sam hanging around the pontoons two days before his death."

Peter was pacing up and down in front of the whiteboards. When he realised what he was doing, he took a deep breath and calmed himself. "Nikki, when you collect our victim's mother tomorrow find out what, if anything, she knew about his previous career; and what he had been doing out here apart from working for the Heritage Group."

"Will do. I talked to his former Chief of Police, who told me he had been a particularly good officer. They were all incredibly surprised when he handed in his resignation, and he didn't even work his months' notice. He took long service leave and was out here within two weeks."

"Could he tell you what he was working on?"

"Yes, Sir. He told me that Sam Heartland had been infiltrating a smuggling ring. He had been feeding back useful information that was leading to arrests being made in London. We all know that this sort of thing does happen from time to time if an officer is working on a case for an extended period, they can just burn out and want to leave."

"Thank you, Nikki. Robert, could you please tell us what happened yesterday."

"We went to the second cave, and at the back of the main chamber we found a passageway that led us underground, back to near the lighthouse. We didn't recover anything from the main entry chamber or the passageway. Inshore Rescue took two of their boats back there for us at high tide. They told me that the larger of their two crafts easily fitted in the main chamber and the tunnel entrance was only three feet away from the bow of their boat. That was when they saw a large, rusted ring attached to the side of the cave wall. They informed me that it could easily be used as a mooring point, but it would be very tricky if there was harsh weather with rough seas. Later in the afternoon, we did a sweep of Sam's room in the share house. No sign of a phone, computer, passport, or a wallet. We did find a membership card for the coin collectors' club, and two more photographs of the coins. The lab has confirmed the photographs are a match for the coins of the stolen collection."

"Anna?"

"Sir, presently we have nothing on Sam. He has a mobile phone registered to him which we know has not been recovered, and still no computer. The coin club have confirmed he was a member and they said he joined within days of arrival at Linley Cove. He managed to get the job with the Heritage a month after settling here." "Well, that's enough information to digest. We need to question all the members of the coin club. Ken, can you organise a couple of cameras to be set up for us? One looking at the seaward side of the cave and the other looking at the grate in the field, behind the light. I don't want you seen whilst you are setting them up and I do not want the cameras to be seen once in position either. Make sure you keep your overtime sheets up-to-date, and I will see you in the morning. Thank you, everyone."

Kev was visiting all the charity and antiques shops in town. Once a week, normally on Saturday mornings, he would look around them in the hope of finding old typewriters. He had a small collection of them at home. As a fourteen year old he had been working in a butcher's shop after school, the shop owner used an old typewriter to write up the accounts after he had closed for the day. Whilst Kev was cleaning up the shop or scrubbing the block where the meat was chopped throughout the day for customers or the display window, he found the sound of the keys being hit and the ding when the page was reset very calming. And when he got around to hoovering and dusting the office area, he always paid the most attention and care to the typewriter in the middle of the large oak desk. He would dust the keys and marvel at the inner workings of the machine. In his opinion, they were incredible works of engineering and mini works of art. Years later, he saw a typewriter like the one his boss had used, and he bought it. That was the start of his collection.

Today, when he was leaving a shop, Kev looked up and saw Liz coming towards him. She had her arm linked to an older lady's arm. He was going to cross the road and pretend not to have seen her as he didn't want to intrude on her time with the older lady. But Liz saw him and waved. Kev waved back and started to walk towards them. When they were quite close together Liz unlinked her arm, gave Kev a hug, and kissed him on the cheek.

"Mum, let me introduce Kevin, my friend from work. The one I went out with last night."

"Good morning, Kevin. Nice to meet you," said Liz's mother, holding out her hand. Kev shook her hand gently. Her hands were long and a bit frail looking, but overall she was a very graceful looking lady. Her long, slim neck and high cheek bones reminded him of a depiction of Nefertiti he had seen once. "Everyone calls me Betty; would you like to join us for lunch?

Every Saturday we go over there for fish and chips. You are most welcome if you have the time."

"Yes, please do!" said Liz.

"Only if you're sure."

"Yes, please do. Liz will only be talking my ears off about you, like she has been doing since waking this morning! So, it will be good to see if you are the wonderful man she tells me you are."

Liz linked her arms with Kev and her mum, and they made their way to the shop. The front of the shop looked like any other chip shop front, but if you went around the corner to the side door it opened into a small but genuinely nice restaurant, decorated with sea-themed paintings on every wall. Once they were seated inside, the waiter took their order and brought their drinks.

"What are you shopping for, Kev?", Liz enquired.

"Oh, it may sound strange, but If I'm not at work on Saturday mornings I look for old typewriters."

"Do you write, then?"

"I do from time to time, but not on a typewriter. I collect and repair them as a hobby."

"Cool! We have two old ones at home. I don't know if they are the sort you'd be able to repair, but would you mind looking at them for us one day? I love to write when I cannot sleep."

"That's when I write, although nothing serious normally. Being dyslexic doesn't help, but I manage to get all the thoughts out of my head so I can go to sleep with a clear mind. And the other thing we have in common is that I come here every Saturday for lunch as well, but normally later than this."

At that point, their food arrived and they all began to eat. Every now and again, Kev would catch Betty looking at the two of them. She was clearly enjoying her meal, and by her expression he could see that she was enjoying seeing Liz so happy in his company.

Peter met up with Paul's parents and Suzie for lunch at the Yacht Club. After a very hearty meal, they took their drinks to the deck overlooking the harbour. After taking a sip of his beer, David asked Peter if anyone had released any information to the press that they did not know about. "No," replied Peter. "Nothing's been released to the press yet, why? "

"I had a call this morning from a yacht broker from London, who wanted to know if *Seabreeze* was for sale."

"We have a connection to the case in London," said Peter, "so I'll follow that up. Could you give me their name and the phone number?"

"I only know the name, not the number. It was Jones and Son, and it was Mr Jones that called me."

"Okay. And you know you cannot sell her whilst the investigation is in progress?"

"Yes, of course. I wouldn't sell her anyway, even if I could. I know Paul will come back to us, so I'm keeping it for him."

Suzie stood and took her drink to the railings on the outskirts of the deck. Turning back to face her parents and Peter, she said, "Anything you can tell us?"

"No, I'm sorry. We are doing the best we can, I promise you

all. It's taking a long time for you, and I'm sorry about that. You will be the first to know anything that I can tell you. I don't want to give you any misleading information, as it is changing all the time now. Regarding the media, on Monday we hope to get a positive identification on the victim, and if he is the person we think he is, then we will be making a statement to the media after that. We will have to release a picture of Paul to them, as a person of interest, and they will say that we need to talk to him as a possible witness."

Suzie became excited and came back to the chair she had been sitting on. "So are you sure that Paul had nothing to do with the man's death?"

"No, hold on, Suzie. Paul at this time is still our main suspect. But we will tell the media that he may be a witness, instead of a suspect so you won't have them camped outside your house for the rest of our investigation. I have a head and shoulder photograph of Paul that I can use for the press, that is unless you want me to use one of your own photos. Let me know before Monday, and I will have it picked up."

Peter looked at Suzie and nodded towards the railings. She took the hint and started heading towards them. Peter followed, with his drink in hand.

"Are you okay?", Peter asked her.

"Yes, just a little stressed."

"Yes, I know. Can I ask you a question?"

"Of course, if you think I can help."

"Do you know what Paul had in his safety deposit box?"

"Well, of course I do! He gave me the contents on Saturday when we had lunch."

"Suzie, why didn't you tell me that?"

"Oh, sorry! That would have been important, wouldn't it?"

"Yes, Suzie it is!", Peter put his drink down heavily on the nearest table and walked around the table with his hands holding the top of his head. Taking a deep breath, he calmed himself. "Suzie, please, what did he give you and why?"

"I'm sorry, Peter. I didn't think. It was his passport, a few insurance policies, his will, and a couple of maps." "Nothing else?"

"No, that's everything from his box. He did also ask me later to look after his laptop. He just said he didn't want to leave it on *Seabreeze* for the rest of the day, as someone had been hanging around the boats and a handful had been broken into recently."

"Thank you. That's good. Don't worry. It's all going to be okay," Peter assured her.

After the morning briefing earlier, Ken went straight to the photographic department. He asked the officer behind the desk to get him two sets of the latest CCTV cameras, stating they must be infra-red for night or daytime recording. He signed the log and was given the cameras, along with a toolbox which contained all the tools needed to fit the cameras to just about any surface. He headed to his car with the three cases and drove to the lighthouse. When he got there, he saw Robert and Eric collecting their field bags from the back of the van.

"Hi guys, long time no see," he said.

Eric looked at his watch. "We were at the briefing with you an hour ago."

"Never mind Eric!", Robert smiled. "Well, the boss said that I shouldn't be seen setting up these cameras, so don't tell on me, will you?"

"We have not set eyes on you at all," Robert said.

Eric was looking at the two of them with a puzzled expression on his face. Robert and Ken nodded to each other, and Ken started walking to the field at the back of the light.

"Come on, Eric, let's do this," said Robert. "I'm sure we have missed something."

They went to the lighthouse, where Robert removed the lock.

It took Ken nearly twenty minutes to find the grate within the field. As soon as he found it he put the coordinates of this spot into his phone. Ken then got down on his knees and opened the grate. He looked around and was certain he couldn't be seen by anyone due to the cover of low bushy plants surrounding the grate. He spent five minutes working out the best position for the first camera, then he worked for a whole hour to fit it and set it up.

Time to test it. He opened the app on his phone and climbed out of the hole, making sure he stayed crouching down just in case anyone was around. He sat on the side of the opening, leaned forward, and turned on the camera. Then he dangled his left leg into the hole. Within twenty seconds, his phone pinged and there was a small, still image of his boot. A message under the displayed image said camera one activated at eleven zero one, Linley Cove lighthouse! '*Okay*,' he thought, '*I had better get onto the next one.*' He was not looking forward to walking down that path to the cave. It was going to be a long and slippery one at times, as they had found out the day before. And that had been walking up the path to the grate, not down as he was about to do.

Ken knew he wouldn't be able to position a camera facing the seaward side of the cave entrance, so the camera recording the entrance would have to be inside the cave. Half an hour later, he had found an acceptable position for the second camera. It was reached from a ledge he could walk along at the tunnel level on the left-hand side of the cave, above the water line. He just had to secure it now, and make sure it couldn't be seen. It took a further hour and a half to secure the camera. When he was sure it was going to be all right, he made a call to Inshore Rescue.

"Hi, this is police photographer Ken Hill. I need a favour."

"Hi, Ken. This is Mark, the coxswain. I was with you the other day. What can we do for you?"

"Well, I can't tell you why, but I will need one of your boats to access the cave again tonight, if weather permits."

"Oh, let me look at the tide. Yes, I'm sure I can have a crew there at eight thirty pm. Will that be okay?"

"Yes, thank you. If anything changes your end, let me know via the switchboard and we'll arrange another time. Can you ask your crew to look out for anything strange when entering, I need to know if they see anything reflecting light or anything that has a visible red hue to it?"

"Will do. Take care."

Ken took a final look around before heading up the path back to the grate. Just as he left the passageway, his phone pinged and showed him an image of his full body facing away from the camera positioned near the grate, along with a message saying camera one had activated at Linley Cove Lighthouse. Hopefully, camera two would give him the same clarity of vision when the Inshore Rescue boat activated it later that night.

Robert and Eric stood side by side after entering the door of the lighthouse.

"Eric. You take the right side, and I'll do the left. We'll walk in time with each other and check out every inch of the inside of the lighthouse, okay?"

Eric nodded his affirmation. They took the first step then the second.

"I can do this, Robert," Eric said when he saw Robert looking to his right side as well as the left.

"Okay, sorry."

They continued to the first rung of the stairs in line together. Ground and first floor completed, they then had to walk in single file as the stairway had narrowed enough that they were now rubbing shoulders. They continued in silence, both looking intently, Robert at the steps and the railings and Eric at the walls.

When they got to the fourth floor, Eric said, "Blood splatter."

"Yes! Let's give this area a really good look, Eric."

Eric thought for a moment. "Our victim was hit on the right-hand side of the head, so with the stairs this narrow the assailant must have been below the victim. But if that person was right-handed, as was Paul according to Peter, then I can't see it."

"Okay, yes. Then let's try to re-enact this, Eric. I'll go up six steps and you go down, then we'll come together, and you can take a swing with a pretend hammer-length object. Use your torch."

They got into position and Robert called out, "Now!"

Within two steps, they both were aware of each other's presence. Robert picked up his pace as he came down the stairs; and Eric, holding the torch aloft in his right hand, also sped up. As they got near enough to each other, Eric swung the torch, trying to connect with the right side of Robert's head.

"There isn't enough room, and you can easily defend yourself. If we reverse our positions so the victim is hit from above, then a right-handed person would have hit our victim on the left side of his head. You wouldn't chance using your non-dominant hand if you were trying to incapacitate someone, let alone trying to kill them. And look at the height of the blood splatter. The victim was six feet tall – he must have been on his knees. Look – I'm only five-five, but if I get down here on my knees." And that's when Eric noticed the founding stone for the extension of the new part of the lighthouse three steps down from the doorway on this fourth floor level.

"Look, Sir," he said. He sat down on the step and Robert looked over his shoulder.

"Bloody hell, Eric, you're on fire today! And look at your position. I think our victim was sitting where you are now, and the assailant has come up the steps and before he could get up to defend himself, he was hit by a left-handed assailant."

They studied the stone. The writing on the top section was deeper and could clearly be read, but the bottom couple of lines were faded or edged less deeply in the stone than the top lines.

"Sir, I could make a rubbing?"

Eric pulled out a folded A4 sheet of paper from one pocket and a pencil from another. Robert held the paper over the stone as Eric gently rubbed the side of the pencil from side to side. All the words were more visible when they appeared on the paper.

"Well done, Eric. You have found it!"

CHAPTER NINE

SUNDAY

"KEN, DID YOU GET the cameras in place?", Peter asked.

"Yes, Sir, at the grate end, after fitting that one. When I came back out of the tunnel, I had a notification on my phone with a clear image of the whole back of my body, by the time I had left the ground. I got another notification at eight thirty last night showing an image of the Inshore Rescue boat entering the cave from the sea. I could clearly see the crew members' faces when I zoomed in on the image from the camera, Sir. I couldn't position a camera facing the entrance as I would have needed to be halfway down the cliff, which I couldn't do; and anyway, I wouldn't have been able to hide its position sorry, Sir. On the plus side Sir, the boats crew, did not say they saw the camera I had positioned".

"Good job. Well done Ken. Now, Robert What have you got for us today?"

Robert stood. "Sorry, Sir, this briefing from my team belongs to Eric. He found all the evidence yesterday. I think he should present."

"Okay, Eric, please tell us what you have found."

"Thank you, Sir and Robert. Yesterday, we went back to the light but did not see Ken." Ken and Robert looked at each other, raised their eyebrows and smiled. "We entered the lighthouse and searched it again, and we discovered two things. One, we do not think Paul could have killed Sam, as he is a right-hander, and the evidence strongly points at a left-handed person committing this crime. And two, we have a rubbing of an inscription at the bottom of the second founding stone, which was laid when the light was extended. We think this inscription was inscribed on to the stone later, under the bit that reads *Laid by the honourable so and so*. It reads: *Second cave shines like gold when lit by the full moon. A calm high tide you need.*"

Peter raised his hand fingers closed together a sign for no one to talk. Turning to Sara he asked her to update Fe after the meeting "I will Sir. Sara was a civilian but always referred to him as Sir when they were in the company of any police personnel. "Now Shani, get this modelled by the computer techs. Make sure what Eric and Robert think about the first injury being caused by a left- or right-handed person. Then show the modelling to Doctor Malloy and see if he confirms."

"Will do, Sir."

"Excellent work, Eric. Anna, how did we do with the fifteen members of the coin club?"

Anna stood, "Well, all but two have been questioned. The missing two were Paul and the victim Sam. Out of the other thirteen, twelve all have alibis. Mr Pomeroy, the Chairperson, is the only one without an alibi, so we are going to talk to him further, and get a warrant to search his house today if possible."

"Fantastic work, all of you. Lastly, a couple of things. David had a call yesterday from a yacht broker in London. The company is called Jones and Son. Find out why or how they have heard *Seabreeze* is up for sale, even though it is not. And I have found out that Suzie has the contents of Paul's safety deposit box. Apparently, he was going to change banks on Monday so he wanted the stuff out of that bank; but he wanted it kept safe for the weekend, so he left it all with her. Let's get that picked up and get the lab to go through it. Ken, find out when the next full moon is and make sure you are with the inshore rescue to check out that cave again from the seaward side."

"Yes Sir I will."

"Let's solve this soon. Thank you, everyone. Oh, before you all go – make sure you leave as soon as you can today, have some time with your families. Anna, you are collecting our victim's mum today? Please don't forget to ask those questions, will you?"

"No, Sir, I won't forget thank you."

At two fifty five, Nikki was at the airport arrivals lounge. When the passengers came through the gate, she held up a sign which simply read, "Mrs HEARTLAND". A lady who looked around the age of seventy approached her.

"Hello, dear. Are you the detective officer I'm meant to be meeting?"

"If you are Mrs Heartland, then I am. No Mr Heartland with you?"

"Yes, I am. I'm sorry, dear, it's been a very long flight, and no there is not a Mr Heartland with me."

"Well, it's nice to meet you. My name is Nikki, and I am your liaison officer for the duration of your stay. So come with me, and we can collect your cases and get you to the hotel so you can rest a little."

Mrs Heartland placed her arm in Nikki's, gave a shrug and said, "You lead and I will follow, dear."

After collecting her case they went to the car, and within an hour they had arrived at the hotel, checked in and went straight up to her room. Nikki opened the door for her.

"Would you like a cup of tea?"

"Thank you. That would be lovely. Milk and two sugars, please." Nikki put the kettle on while Mrs Heartland started to unpack.

Nikki also phoned the on-call Mortuary tech as she waited for the tea to brew. She arranged a viewing of the patient with Coroner's Number 321C105 for the next day.

When the tea was ready, she placed the cup on the table in front of the settee where Mrs Heartland was now sitting.

"There you go. If you don't mind, I just need to ask you a few questions before I leave you."

"Ask away, dear. You are such a sweet girl; I will help you with anything I can."

"Thank you. Well, firstly, did you know what your son did for work before he came out here?"

"Oh, yes. He was a particularly good police officer. He was so good he didn't have to wear a uniform. Just like you; you look so smart in your suit. I'm not meant to know this, but he did undercover work."

"Do you know what sort of case he was working on before he left the service?"

"I'm not going to get in trouble, am I? I'm not meant to know."

"No, you're not in any trouble. If you can help us, we will be able get the answers that you need, and help you come to terms with what has happened to your son."

"Okay, dear, as long as it's you I have to talk to and not some big hairy sergeant."

Nikki laughed. "Course not, not at all. All the time you are here, I am the only officer you will talk to."

"I knew it had something to do with smuggling and coins. Sam loved collecting coins. Do you know that the old ones sell for vast amounts of money? Those Roman ones have sold for thousands of pounds."

"Okay. Do you know how Sam managed to leave his job and be able to work here as soon as he did after leaving?"

"I was surprised that he left. Especially when he was working on a case that involved coins. We had dinner together on a Saturday night and he told me he was going to leave the job. And he wanted me to come and live here as well. We're citizens, you know; we both have dual passports. When Sam was around two years old his father worked in the mines here, and we relocated. After a while, he said we should become citizens for tax reasons, which we did; but when the silly sod went off with a younger girl I went back to London with Sam. We never got divorced and I have not seen him or had any contact with him since. Sam's last case was mainly centred in and around here, and he would come back to London once a month and go to work to see his boss, spend a couple of days with me, then come back here. I think being over here for so much time, he just missed the place and maybe wanted to find his father. But he never said that to me."

"Thank you, Mrs Heartland, thank you so much. Now I'm going to leave you to get a little rest. Make sure you get something to eat later. There's a card on the table that tells you what time the restaurant is open this evening and all the times for the rest of the week. Make sure you don't pay for a thing. If someone asks how you'd like to pay, all you say is 'can you charge my room'. The police will pay for your stay, including meals, but only if you have them here. We cannot cover the costs if you eat somewhere else. I'll come back for you at ten thirty tomorrow morning."

"Thank you. Can you see yourself out dear? I am so tired now I don't think I can get up."

"Of course. You take care, I will see you tomorrow."

Peter spent the rest of the morning in his office sorting a fresh pile of paperwork from his in-tray and then he went to the Yacht Club and had lunch. He sat there for a couple of hours, looking over at *Seabreeze*, thinking the case through from the first call to this moment in time.

Ken contacted Inshore Rescue and organised a night trip to the cave for the following Friday at around 10pm. He had found from a search on the internet that the full moon would be at its brightest then. He also called the duty officer of the Police boat and booked their attendance as well. He would need them to be witnesses for any evidence he might find. Also, if anyone else was around, he would have back-up.

In the morning, Robert and Eric met up with Suzie and recovered Paul's laptop and the documents she had. They returned them to the lab for a thorough forensic examination, then they both went home to their families.

Anna met a couple of police officers outside Pomeroy's house. She told them that she was there to exercise a warrant to search the house, and she needed to interview him. She rang the doorbell and they stood there for thirty seconds or so before a voice called out from the end of the drive.

"Hello, can I help you?"

"Are you Mr Pomeroy?"

"Yes. Yes, I am. What can I do for you, officers?"

"We have a warrant which enables us to enter your house. Also I need to question you in connection with an investigation we are conducting into the possible murder of Sam Heartland, a person we know you knew."

Pomeroy looked over both shoulders to see if any of his neighbours were watching from their windows, or if anyone was in their garden or on the street and could have heard the officer. "Yes," he said. "Yes, come in. I've got nothing to hide." He rushed past them to the front door, then ushered them into the house as quickly as he could.

He relaxed a bit once he was inside. Anna explained that they were going to search his house and that afterwards he would be cautioned, and a recorded interview would take place witnessed by the two police officers. Pomeroy agreed and they proceeded to search each room, with him close on their heels.

CHAPTER TEN

MONDAY

KEV ARRIVED AT WORK early, entering the tea room he put the kettle on before noticing Joe asleep on the settee. He scanned the room carefully looking for cans. Checking the bin, he counted six empty cans of stout. Noisily, he took the bag out of the bin. He tied it up on his way out of the room, kicking the end of the settee as he passed it.

"JOE! You're an idiot."

Kev took the bag out to the main bin in the loading bay area outside. When he returned, Joe was sitting at the edge of the settee with his head in his hands.

Hearing Kev come into the room, he said, "What? I cleaned up."

"Six cans, Joe!"

"What? That was over the whole weekend. Every time I went to leave, the bloody phone would go off again. Then I would have to hang around for the Daves to come in. We have six new patients – it was crazy."

"Would you like a coffee?", Kev asked.

"Yes, please. Three sugars today, thanks."

Over the next hour, the others came in. Darren was the last to arrive. "Sorry, everyone," he said. "Am I late? That traffic was bad. I think there must have been a crash somewhere and everyone and his wife decided to go my way. Anyway, do you all mind if we have the meeting now?"

Kev looked around the room and answered for all, "Fine by us," he said.

Darren got his diary out of his case and sat on the arm of the settee. Looking up and down the marked page, he said, "Right then, I'm pleased to inform you all that with a recommendation from Kev, Sully is now promoted to eviscerate. Excellent work, Sully. Kev told me he was extremely impressed with the way you conducted yourself and the mindfulness you showed to your patient during your test run. Keep it up, okay?"

The team gave Sully a brief clap. Sully was standing by the window; he patted his own back a couple of times and took an exuberant bow.

"Now Joe, it looks like you had a busy weekend. Are you okay?"

"Umm, I am a bit tired."

"If you want you can give Kev an update about our new patients, and then you can assist Sully. We have three autopsies booked for this morning – unless, that is, you want to be in the office today, Joe?"

"No, I do not."

"Okay, settled. Has anybody anything else to add?" Darren looked around the room. "No? Okay, let's do this. Have a good day." He went to his office.

Kev and Joe followed him out of the room but went to the central office. Sully and the others went to the changing rooms.

Kev and Joe sat down at the large desk and looked at the register. Joe pulled a piece of paper out of his pocket and put it on the desk. Clearing his throat and looking over to the fax machine to make sure, he said, "We haven't received any paperwork from the Coroner on the six new patients, so I don't know what we'll be doing for them yet. A police officer will be coming to identify that unnamed one we have now." He handed Kev the paper.

"Is that 321?", Joe repositioned his glasses and looked at the paper.

"Yes, 321C105."

"What are the extra two numbers, Joe?"

"Oh, that's the time, sorry. Eleven this morning."

"Thanks, Joe. If there's nothing else, you'd better get into the autopsy room with the others." Kev was still a little short with him after finding the cans earlier, and he shook his head as Joe left the room. '*How are you going to end up, Joe?*', he wondered.

Peter entered the incident room. "Morning, everyone. Let's get started. Nikki, how did it go when you picked up Mrs Heartland?"

"Sir, she is a wonderful older lady. I'm going to pick her up at ten thirty this morning to take her to the Mortuary. She was aware that her son was an undercover officer, and she knew that before he quit he was investigating a smuggling gang here. They both have citizenship and lived here when Sam was young, but moved back to the UK after her marriage to his father broke up.

That's how he got to work out here so quickly after leaving the job, Sir."

"Robert, please?"

"Eric and I met up with Suzie and recovered the items from the safety deposit box. The lab has gone through it all and they have not found anything incriminating from those items, or from the laptop, Sir."

"Good. Shani?"

"We took the computer model to the pathologist, and he agrees with Eric that the person we need to look for is left-handed. He concluded that the first wound would have killed him in a short amount of time without immediate medical attention. Instead of getting that help, he either fell or was pushed off the balcony and subsequently died there on the ground. He will officially inform the Coroner today."

"Excellent. Anna?"

Anna stood up. "Sir, we found out that there are no yacht brokers in London with the company name of Jones and Son, so we are a bit stumped about that one. We could put a tap on David and Wendy's home phone if you like?"

"Okay, I'll talk to them about that later. What of our Mr Pomeroy?"

"Very shifty, Sir. We did a search of his house and car. We found more photos of the coins, so we now have all ten photos, the lab has confirmed. We recovered Sam's wallet, phone, and laptop from his spare room. I would love to have arrested him on the spot, but we don't have anything to link him to the murder."

"How did he explain the photographs and being in possession of Sam's things?"

"Sir, he told me that Paul and Sam were particularly good at finding coins in online auction sales around the world. He had found that out after talking to them after one of the club meetings. At the next meeting, he gave them the photos and asked them to try to locate the coins for him just in case someone was trying to sell them online after they were stolen. Paul and Sam didn't know that from him, but I think Sam knew it all along and was still investigating Pomeroy on his own, rather than for the London Met. He said he didn't tell them they were stolen as he was trying to get them back. He wanted to take the credit for finding them on his own, but he needed their help. He explained that he had Sam's stuff because sometimes Sam would go to his house after their meetings, and if they had drinks then Sam would stay over. That's why his stuff was there; he'd stayed on the Saturday night. But he said that Sam wasn't there on Sunday morning when he woke up."

"Now, Ken did you make the call you were going to make?"

"Yes, Sir. I am going to meet up with Inshore Rescue and the police boat, and they will take me to the cave for ten on Friday night. I have had no sightings of anyone from the cameras so far."

"Steve and Andy, can you investigate the finances of the coin club and for Mr Pomeroy, please? I hope you did get time with your families yesterday. I am doing a segment for tonight's news so I'm heading to the TV station this morning to see if we can get the viewers' help in finding Paul. Then I will catch up with David and Wendy. See you all in the morning."

The office in the Mortuary was surprisingly quiet for a Monday morning. Kev had just finished another coffee. He looked up at the clock and went to get the patient from the fridge. He positioned the hand pump hydraulic trolley at the very centre of the opened fridge bay door, raising and lowering the pump several times until the trolley was almost level with the tray on which the patient was lying. Then he pulled the tray out about an arm's length from the fridge and raised the trolley a little more, so the underside of the tray touched the first roller on the trolley. Pressing the brake with his foot, he confidently pulled the tray completely out of the fridge. After releasing the brake, Kev moved the trolley away from the fridge and closed the fridge door with his foot. The reassuring sound of a click confirmed that the door was closed.

Kev unwrapped the sheet at the level of the patient's wrist, to find the ID band. He did not find it there so he looked on the other wrist, and there it was. He made a mental note to himself to mention this at the morning meeting. 'It would be a good idea,' he thought, 'if everyone in future placed the identification tags in the same position always.' After checking the number on the wrist band with the number on the board again, he pushed the trolley to the viewing room fridge bay side entrance.

Peter pulled into the multi-storey carpark next to the TV station building. He got all the way to level five before he could find a park. Four minutes later, he was at the reception desk in the vast expanse of the foyer.

"Hi, I'm Peter. I have an interview booked with a Mr Presley."

The receptionist looked at the computer screen to her side. "Oh yes, there you are. If you use the south lifts over there, go up to level four and turn left when you exit, go to the end of the corridor, and turn right, Mr Presley will be there."

"Thankyou."

Peter turned and headed for the lift. At level four, he got out and turned left, walked to the end of the corridor, and then turned right. This place was much bigger than he remembered. He had only been to this network's station a couple of times over the years and had been sent to various parts of the building, so this part of the building was all new to him.

He was now facing two large wooden doors. He pushed the left side open and was greeted by a short, balding man who was holding a clipboard and wearing a headset. The man immediately raised a finger to his lips then held up his entire hand with all his fingers closed together. Peter nodded and stayed where he was. A couple of minutes later, the man tucked the clipboard under his arm and again held up his hand to Peter. This time he started closing each finger down and mouthing the words. Five, four, three, two, one. Then he gave Peter a thumbs-up using both hands.

"Sorry about that. We were live on air, so if you had made one sound I would have been sacked. How can I help you?" he said.

"I'm Peter. I have an interview with Mr Presley."

"Oh yes, the detective. Come with me."

The man showed Peter to a comfortable leather-bound chair and scurried away. A short time later, an exceptionally large, stocky man came striding towards Peter. His voice boomed out across the TV studio.

"Peter, good to see you again. How's life?"

Peter stood and shook his hand. "Presley! I'm good, thank you, but I am a bit pressed for time."

"Yes. Yes of course you are, please take a seat. So, you know the drill. Just look at me and tell me what you can about this missing man of yours and we will get him found. Don't worry about the cameras – they'll work around you. And the microphone is hidden in that plant next to you."

Peter repositioned himself on the seat and said, "Okay, thank you."

Presley held his hand up to his ear and pushed his earpiece further in. He looked around the room and his voice boomed out again. "Did you get that?"

A technician standing behind one of the three cameras made himself visible and gave a thumbs up. Presley boomed, "Good! Then let us begin. In your own time, Peter."

Nikki arrived outside the hotel room and knocked twice on the door. A little voice called out, "Hello, who is it?"

Nikki called back, "Good morning, Mrs Heartland. It's Nikki. I collected you from the airport yesterday."

"Oh, good morning, my dear," Mrs Heartland was saying as she opened the door. "Please come in. I've just got to get my bag and I will be ready."

"No rush. We have time," Nikki replied.

Mrs Heartland went off immediately to get her bag from the bedroom. Nikki called after her, "Did you get dinner last night, Mrs Heartland?"

"Yes, I did. It was so nice. They are really looking after me here. I had dinner and a glass of sherry, and then a nice young girl from reception brought me back to the room."

"It's good to hear they are looking after you. Shall we go?" Nikki said.

Patting her handbag with her right hand, Mrs Heartland answered, "Yes, I am all ready. Let's get this out of the way then I can buy you lunch."

"I'm not sure about that," Nikki replied. "Let's see how you are after."

"Oh, please, dear. It will be my treat."

"We'll see. Come on, let's go."

Seconds later, they were halfway down the corridor approaching the lifts. Mrs Heartland placed her arm through Nikki's. Minutes later they had reached Nikki's unmarked police car, which she had conveniently left right outside the main foyer. Nikki opened the left-hand side back door for Mrs Heartland and closed it gently once she was in the car.

In the viewing room, Kev had just finished putting a new bandage on the patient's head, as the one Sully had put on before was stained with blood, that had leaked from the wound since the first viewing. He looked around the room and nodded, happy that he had presented the patient in the best way. On the way back to the office, he took off his gloves at the sink and placed them in the bin, which was lined with a yellow biohazard bag, and washed his hands. He entered the office and took a drink from his water bottle. Just then the phone rang, he put the bottle on the side cabinet and picked up the receiver.

"Mortuary, Kev speaking. How can I help you?"

"Morning, Kev. This is Nikki. I have Mrs Heartland with me in your waiting room. We are here to carry out an identification on one of your patients."

"Yes, of course. Please take a seat and I will be right with you."

"Thank you, Kev." Nikki replaced the receiver and returned to sit next to the now very frail-looking woman sitting in the corner of the room.

"Are you okay, Mrs Heartland?"

"Yes, thank you. Although I could do with a glass of water, if you don't mind?"

"Of course." Nikki went to the water cooler behind the door and pulled out a paper cup and filled it halfway. The machine made a gurgling noise and bubbles rose from the bottom of the machine to the top. She returned to the seat, where she held onto the cup until she was sure Mrs Heartland had a firm enough grip on it.

"Thank you, dear," she said before taking a sip.

There was a knock on the door and Kev entered the room and introduced himself. He sat opposite them and said, "Before we go in, I need to give you a bit of information. Firstly, I need to make sure you are coming in to see Mr Heartland, who has Coroner's Reference Number 321C105."

Nikki opened the last page of her notepad and confirmed the number.

"Good. I also must inform you that the patient we have in the viewing room has a significant wound on the right side of his head, which I have covered with a bandage." Kev noticed the older lady clutch onto the detective's hand. "The patient is lying on top of a barouche with his head on a pillow, and I have placed a green quilt over the top of him which extends from his shoulders to past his feet. The lighting is about the same as in this room, but I can make it brighter if you wish. I will wait for you outside the viewing room door, so please come through when you are ready."

Kev got up from the chair and made his way to the door outside the viewing room. He always positioned himself here when conducting a viewing, as it meant that he could open the door for the visitors entering or leaving the room. He was able to hear, and see, the people once they were inside, as he never fully closed the door. The patient inside the room was still under Kev's care, and he needed to keep an eye on the proceedings. By being close to the official, that had come in with the family, he was able to help them in case emotions escalated. It was good also to be on hand to help answer any questions for them if the official did not know or gave wrong information. All this had to be done discretely and with as little imposition as possible.

One minute later, Mrs Heartland and the detective were coming towards him. He opened the door and moved back so he was against the wall. The old lady was using both her hands to hold onto the detective's arm as they got closer to him.

"Take your time," Kev said, "and in my experience it helps to take in a deep breath before you enter."

The detective nodded and Mrs Heartland let out a broken, "Thank you."

Nikki released Mrs Heartland's grip from her arm as it was

starting to hurt. Instead, she took hold of her left hand. Nikki passed her a tissue and Mrs Heartland wiped a tear away.

"Sorry, dear, I'm ready."

They entered the room and the older lady started to sob. Nikki let go of her hand and put her arm around Mrs Heartland's shoulders.

"Yes! This is my precious boy." She bent down and kissed him on the forehead. "Goodbye, son, see you in heaven." She turned and started to leave, then at the door she turned back towards him and blew him a kiss. "Can we go now, please?"

"If you're sure. You can stay as long as you like."

"No, I'm sure."

Kev and the detective nodded to each other. No words needed to be said. They both were feeling upset for the old lady to have to go through this experience. Kev waited until they were out of the corridor before pulling out a pair of gloves from his pocket. He put them on and set about returning the patient to the fridge bay.

Peter arrived at Paul's parents' house at twelve thirty-five. "Afternoon, David. I have news. Can I come in?" "Please do."

They sat down in the lounge and were shortly joined by Wendy and Suzie. Peter stood up when they came in and gave them each a hug, then sat down again and shuffled to the edge of the seat.

"I have good news for you all. My team have discovered that Paul did not kill anyone that we know of, so he is no longer a suspect in the murder. I have given an interview this morning to the ACC, and they will air that on tonight's news. Hopefully, we'll get loads of calls from the public overnight, and maybe someone knows Paul's whereabouts."

Suzie clapped her hands. "Oh, God! I do hope so."

David and Wendy stood and gave each other a hug. Tears running down their cheeks, they turned to Peter and thanked him. When Suzie came across the room with a beaming smile on her face, Peter stood up and she gave him a hug and a kiss.

Wendy put her hand on her chest and with tears in her eyes said, "It will be so good to see him again. And to know that he's not in trouble with the police is a great relief. Thank you, Peter."

"One more thing before I go. With your permission, I would like to put a bug in your phone in case the broker from London calls again. We would like to speak with him as there is no listed company called Jones and Son, so by using a bug we'll be able to trace the call back to its location."

David looked at Wendy and shrugged his shoulders, and both nodded.

David walked Peter to the door, leaving Wendy and Suzie hugging each other.

"You take care, David," said Peter. "I'll get that tap on your phone organised. Bye."

CHAPTER ELEVEN

TUESDAY

IN THE INCIDENT ROOM, Peter was reviewing all the information on the six large white boards, which now ran the length of the left-hand wall. He was checking off the information against what he had written in his notebook. He used a new notebook every time he started a case. Eventually, the notebook would be put in a plastic Ziplock bag and sealed with evidence tape signed and dated by him, then placed in a box file in the evidence room with all the other documents relating to that case. If this case needed to be studied by anyone in the future or ended up as an unsolved case, then the investigation could be reviewed at any time, and the officers reviewing it would have a clear insight to the leading detectives' thoughts and the processes they followed.

Anna approached Peter, "Morning, Sir. Everything in order?"

"Good morning, Anna. Yes, you've done an excellent job keeping up to date with the boards, well done."

"Thank you, Sir. I need to let you know Shani has just texted me to say she'll be a few minutes late for the briefing. She had a call relating to the case and is following it up now before she attends."

"Thanks Anna. That's fine."

Peter finished checking his notes against the last board and looked up at the clock. It was eight twenty seven. He put the notebook in his right inside breast pocket of his jacket, picked up his bag and entered his office. He checked his watch with the office clock, opened his computer, and started reviewing the extensive list of new emails in his inbox. He was looking at the screen, but he was not reading; he was thinking. He was proud of himself, getting this far in his career. He had reached the same rank as his father before him. It was a lonely job. Early on in his career, he had found it difficult not to micromanage a team he had put together. When he was going out with Suzie, he had been in that state of mind. He would stay in his office until the team had left for the day, and then spend hours in the quiet, checking for himself the information they had given him. He would be at work from six in the morning till late in the evening every day. When Suzie left him, Peter had six appointments with the forces counselling service, and over time had learnt to trust himself to pick a good team, and then to trust them to do the best they could. He wondered if he and Suzie could get back together again. To his knowledge, she had not been in another relationship and was always pleased to see him.

He jumped when he heard the knock on his door.

"Sorry to interrupt. It's just gone nine, Sir."

Peter looked up at Sara. "Yes, I'm coming. Thank you, Sara."

He followed her out of the office.

"Thank you, everyone. Sorry for the delay," he said to the gathered team. "Let's begin with Andy and Steve, please."

Andy stood up. "Sir, we investigated the accounts of the coin club yesterday. Clean as a whistle. The same with Mr Pomeroy."

"Thank you, Andy. Nikki, please tell us what happened at the Mortuary."

"Mrs Heartland has positively identified the victim as her son, Sam Heartland. I stayed with her for a couple of hours afterwards. She was broken."

At that moment, the door swung open making a loud thud as it hit the doorstop. Everyone turned to see a very red-faced Shani hopping through the doorway.

"Sorry, everyone," she said. "My heel broke and I fell against the door." As she spoke, she bent her lower leg up behind her and unstrapped the offending shoe and held it in her left hand. She then lifted the other leg and took off the heeled shoe. Standing just inside the doorway in bare feet, she apologised again.

With a half-smile on his face, Peter said, "Well, now you are with us, would you like to tell us what development you have?"

Shani put her shoes down, and fanning her face with one hand, said, "Yes, I would. thank you. We have found Paul!"

Everyone spontaneously began to clap for nearly a whole minute.

"A nurse from Maryland Hospital in New South Wales phoned us in the early hours, after seeing the late news. She told an officer that a man resembling Paul's picture had been a patient of hers for the last four days. I found out that the local police failed to circulate his picture leading to it not being flagged on the system.

He had been found on a local beach, unconscious and with no identification, and he was taken to the hospital. He was given scans and had surgery for a broken arm and a head injury; he was then placed in an induced coma to allow the brain swelling to subside. We have a ninety-eight percent match on facial recognition from the photo she sent me this morning. The good news, Sir, is that they are bringing him out of the coma today and expect him to make a full recovery. He is in a side room, and I have asked the local police to give him a formal interview as soon as he is awake and able to talk.

An officer will be outside his room from now on, and they will report directly to me." Peter let out a sigh. "Thank you, Shani. I'll inform his parents as soon as I can this morning. I am sure they will want to visit, and they will be able to formally identify him for us. From the injuries he has sustained, I suspect he was at the light at the same time as Sam, and the person or persons that did this had to leave Sam there as he was dead already. I think they may have captured and abducted Paul after seeing him. Until we are a hundred percent sure, we will not release this to the press. So no one is to utter a word outside of these four walls. Robert, can you update us now?"

"Sir, we put the tap on David and Wendy's phone, and Ken has put up a couple of extra cameras in the harbour and at the lighthouse, to cover some large blind spots we identified from the council system of cameras." "Good. Anna?"

"The team and I have been monitoring the calls to David's house and we are reviewing the footage of the new cameras, but have got nothing so far."

Darren had texted Kev to say he was attending a meeting, and asked if he would mind organising the day for the others. Kev walked into the tea room,

"Morning all Darren's not here this morning, so. Bianca and Alison, could you both be in the office please. Sully, Mike, and Joe, could you look after the autopsies. And before we get on, would you all take a vote on an idea I've had. I think it would be good to standardise the positioning of name tags on our patients. What I am proposing is that we put the wrist band on the right wrist and the ankle tag on the left ankle, assuming the patient has got a right wrist and left ankle! If they don't, then we use what we can." There was a moment of discussion. Mike looked at the others, who nodded, and he answered for all,

"Yes, good idea. It would be handy to know exactly where the tags will be."

"Good, so everyone agrees. Thank you. I will update the funeral directors and the two Daves, and I'll change the diagram on the fridge room wall. If anybody wants to raise anything else, feel free." They all looked at each other and shook their heads. "Okay, thank you, everyone. Have a great day."

As soon as he could leave the office, Peter rushed round to see David and Wendy. Suzie opened the door.

"Are your mum and dad in?"

"Yes, in the garden."

Peter pecked her on the cheek, grabbed her hand, and started heading for the back door.

"Wow, hold on – the door!" Suzie released his hand and went back to close the front door.

Peter waited for her to come back and picked up her hand again. "Come on," he said, "I have very good news."

"Have you found him?"

"I've got to tell you all at the same time. Come."

Suzie had overtaken Peter by the time they reached the back door but was still holding his hand, and by now was almost running through the open door. She called out, "Mum! Dad! Peter is here and he has news, he has news!"

On hearing this David and Wendy rose from their seats and started heading back to the house. The two couples met almost in the middle of the garden.

"Morning, Peter. What have you got for us?", David asked.

Wendy put her arm through David's and held him tightly. Suzie did the same with Peter, shaking with anticipation at what she thought he was going to say.

"Okay! Okay!", said Peter, his voice a little shaky, "We are almost positive we have found Paul. Listen, it sounds worse than it is."

"For God's sake, tell us!" Suzie said.

"We think Paul is in Maryland Hospital in New South Wales. He has been in an induced coma for the last few days but is being taken out of it today. Now, the doctors believe he will make a full recovery, but it is going to take time."

"Can we see him?", they all said at the same time.

"If you want to, you can go there. There'll be an officer outside his room, and they have been told that if you turn up then only one of you can go in first to give us a positive identification."

"We're going now," David said, receiving enthusiastic nods from Wendy and Suzie.

"Okay," said Peter, "I have to go now. Drive safely do not rush."

Suzie walked with him to the front door, her arm still through his. Before he left, she gave him a lingering kiss on the lips, "Thank you, Peter. I'll call you later."

"You take care, make sure you share the driving. It will take you about five hours, I think."

"We will, I promise. Talk to you later."

Peter left and went back to the office before returning home later.

CHAPTER TWELVE

WEDNESDAY

"MORNING, EVERYONE."

The incident room fell silent.

Peter paced up and down in front of the whiteboards as he spoke.

"David, Wendy, and Suzie left to see Paul just after lunchtime yesterday, and at seven pm David positively identified Paul to the officer posted outside his room. Afterwards the officer was joined by another, and under caution, they conducted a formal interview with Paul. When they had completed the interview, David, Wendy, and Suzie spent an hour or so with him on their own. During the interview, Paul had told the officers that he remembers sitting on the front deck of *Seabreeze* Saturday night. From that position, he can see the front of the lighthouse during daylight, but by this time it was getting dark. He saw a flashlight and movement. He knew he'd left his wallet up there and wouldn't normally have been worried about it, but seeing a light he thought he had better get up there. He grabbed his phone and got there as quickly as he could. He'd had a few drinks of Jim Beam, so he didn't take his motorbike. He said he half ran and half walked to get up there quickly.

"When he got to the gate, he crouched down to catch his breath and to see if he could find out what was going on. He saw three people sneak up to a fourth who was entering through the lighthouse door. They waited for about twenty seconds then followed him in. Paul was going to phone the police at that point, but when he reached for his phone it wasn't in his pocket. It would take too long to get to the nearest phone box, he decided to get closer so he could at least get a description of the people for the police later.

"He hid behind the bushes by the door, waiting for them to come out. He could hear someone moaning in pain and then he heard shouting. The next thing, he saw someone come out onto the balcony. The person leaned on the railing, but it just gave way and they fell. Paul described hearing a sickening thud when the person hit the ground. He said he was afraid but ran over to the man. He was surprised to find it was Sam Heartland. Paul could see his own wallet sticking out of Sam's pocket. He said Sam was motionless on the ground, He got up to get help but remembers nothing after that point until he woke up in the hospital this morning."

Peter paused for a moment before continuing. "So how does this hold up? Maybe we can still find his phone in the area between the boat and the gate of the lighthouse car park. It's unlikely, but it could still be out there. Robert, can you and the others do a sweep?"

"We can, Sir, but first we need to go to *Seabreeze*. About an hour ago, it was reported to have been broken into sometime last night."

"Who reported it?"

"The Yacht Club security guard, Sir. I said we would attend as soon as we could, to see if we could identify anything missing, or to see if we can lift any fresh prints."

Peter nodded his agreement, then asked Anna to get a copy of the last twenty-four hours' footage from all the CCTV cameras and sort through it all.

After the morning meeting in the Mortuary, Darren asked Kev to join him in his office. "Bring your coffee if you like. Let's have a chat."

Kev entered the office and looked around. '*Darren's had a tidy up*,' he thought. When you entered the office, the first thing you normally saw was a round table in the right-hand corner opposite the door, with four chairs around it. That table used to have a load of files all over it but was now totally clear. When you turned to the right, you saw a large desk running from behind the door along the wall, curving around the corner, then continuing along the back wall. This desk, too, normally would have paperwork all over it. The computer in the far-left corner would have post-it notes everywhere, but not now. The two filing cabinets in the right-hand corner had cleared tops, with a couple of models of Ducati motorbikes on them. Darren still owned a real one but hardly ever rode it anymore.

"Take a seat, Kev," said Darren, gesturing to the table. They both sat and took a sip of their coffees.

Putting down his cup, Kev said, "This is a bit clean for you. What is going on?"

"Well, that's what I wanted to talk to you about. It isn't final yet, but I may be leaving. You must not breathe a word of this. Nothing is going to change for the time being. The Board wanted me to ask you if you would like to be the Mortuary Manager if I do leave, if not they will give Alison the opportunity."

"Bloody Hell! That is unexpected. Where are you going?"

"*If,* I'm going," Darren corrected.

"Okay, *if* you go, then where? By the look of your office, it seems you have already made your choice."

"I would be lying if I said I don't think I will take the position if it is offered to me."

"But where, Darren?"

"I have been asked if I could set up a forensic centre in the Northern Territory. I used to live up there as a teenager, so it would be nice to live there again and set up a home before I plan to retire in around six years."

"Well, I'm shocked! And you want me to run this place?"

"It is well above my pay grade, Kev, to decide that. The Board asked me to see if you would be willing, that's all. They know you are capable. They have even said that if you did agree to take it, they would give you full access to the secretary pool upstairs. You know I have paperwork to do for this job. To help you with your dyslexia, they said if you needed anything typed, then they would see it was done for you by Mary or the other secretaries."

Kev took a big gulp of his coffee, "I don't know. I can't think. This is a bit overwhelming for me, right now."

"You have a couple of days, Kev; my next meeting is on Friday afternoon. That's when they want your decision. The other thing I wanted to say to you is a big thank you for basically running this place for me over the last few weeks. I know I have had a lot of days off recently. I want to acknowledge that I have appreciated you stepping up."

Kev finished his coffee and stood up, "Thanks Darren. I need to think about this. I'll talk to you later. Oh, can I ask a favour? Would you mind covering my on-call on Friday night? I would like a chance to catch up with Liz."

"Yes, I had heard that you went on a date. Of course I will. But remember, Friday lunchtime I need your answer." "Will do."

Kev left the room and went outside to the loading bay area, sat down on a wooden crate beside the large cargo bin, and smoked a cigarette. At this time, his main thought about running the Mortuary was that everyone would know that he needed help to do all the correspondence that managers do. They had to review old policies and procedures or write new ones, and then there was all the corresponding with third parties. And being able to have the confidence to help staff be their absolute best. After sitting there for a couple of minutes, he knew deep in his heart that everyone already knew he needed help. Seven years ago, when he sat his final exam, the Royal College let the head of the secretary pool, Mary, be his scribe; and Dr Malloy sat in to make sure she only wrote on the exam paper exactly what Kev answered to the exam question, which she read aloud to him. Kev's initial thoughts were that this promotion should go to Alison.

Kev returned to the Mortuary, wrote a note to Liz, then went to the storeroom to place it on the shelf. When he opened the door at the end of the autopsy room, he nearly jumped out of his skin. Liz was standing right there in front of him.

"Hey, that's rude! I'm not that scary, am I?", Liz said with a pout.

"Oh God. No! I was just going to leave you a note. If you want, I have my Friday night covered so we could go out."

"That would be wonderful. Mum's been talking about you nonstop. Would you mind coming over to my house? You could take a quick look at the typewriters for Mum, to see if you think you'd be able to get them working. They are incredibly special to her, and she would be so grateful if they could work again. Then we could go out."

"No problem. I would love to take a look, and equally, I would love to take you out."

Liz wrapped her arms around him and kissed him on the lips, "Well, give me the note then, and get back to work!"

Kev gave her the note and smiled as he watched her skip out of the storeroom and through the door to her side of the department.

CHAPTER THIRTEEN

THURSDAY

WENDY AND SUZIE WERE walking barefoot along a pristine beach. It was a stone's throw away from the hotel they were now staying at. It was close to the Hospital that Paul was in. They had been lucky to get accommodation, so late in the day, without a prior booking being made. David stayed in the hotel room, instead of joining Wendy and Suzie for their normal pre breakfast walk, he needed to make a couple of calls regarding one of his fishing boats that was being refitted back at Linley Cove.

The sea would occasionally surround Wendy's and Suzie's feet, it was surprisingly cold for this time of year but neither of them minded. They walked and walked in silence, deep in their own thoughts of what had been happening over the last few days. They walked arm in arm, feeling thankful that Paul was going to be okay.

Peter clapped his hands together, "Can someone tell me why

there are so many boxes of chocolates lying around?" Eric, finishing his eighth chocolate since arriving in the incident room five minutes earlier, handed Peter a card. It read:

To the investigation team headed by Peter, thank you so much for finding our son and proving that he could not have been involved in the poor man's death. We hope you enjoy the chocolates. Sent with sincere gratitude,

David, Wendy, Paul, and Suzie xx

"Okay, settle! Don't eat too many of them. I cannot afford to have any of you off sick, especially now. Robert, let's start with you."

Robert screwed up a sheet of A4 paper which contained the wrappers from the chocolates he had consumed. He threw it over Ken's head and when he heard the reassuring sound of it hitting the inside edge of the bin behind Ken, he stood up. "Morning, Sir. Yesterday we went to *Seabreeze* and found a considerable number of new prints inside and outside the yacht, but unfortunately the two individuals that left them have not got a record, so far as we can tell. So no match on the database. Eric decided to take his fish lander net, and surprisingly, he found two mobile phones in the water under the jetty. The tech guys are still trying to dry them out so we can find out who they belong to. Hopefully, one of them will belong to Paul."

"Good work. Ken, can you go through the plan again with the Inshore Rescue and police boat captains today? I have a feeling we're going to get this cracked tomorrow, so I want it watertight."

"Will do, Sir."

"Anna, anything on the CCTV?"

"We do have the two men on the cameras, but considering how careless they were about leaving prints everywhere, they somehow managed to only show part of their faces to the camera."

"Okay. Shani, please."

When she stood, she noticed everyone looking at her shoes, "Yes, thank you." She went red in the face but smiled and continued, "Yes, I am wearing flats, so the door should be safe from me today! Anyway, Sir, from the footage we have, we can tell how tall they are. We have their fingerprints, so when we get them, we will be able to positively identify them and arrest them."

"Good work. Turning to Sara Peter then said. "When we are done here could you take some of these chocolates to the lab staff and pass on my personal thanks for all the late-night work they have been doing for us." "Yes Sir."

"Nikki, how is Mrs Heartland?" "Mrs Heartland is bearing up well, Sir considering. I'm collecting her today and we are going to see a funeral director to start the process of getting her son repatriated back to London."

Kev got up and washed his cup. He was having a conversation with Alison, Bianca, and Mike about their plans for the weekend and they were trying to push him into giving them details about how his relationship with Liz was going. Darren entered and tapped his thigh with his diary, to get everyone's attention, "Kev, I saw your note. You can do the photography this morning, and I'd like you to start instructing Sully in the art of editing and filing the photos. You never know, one day you may decide to leave so we need someone other than Mike to be trained up so they can take over. Now, the rest of you can repeat the same duties you did yesterday. But look at next week's roster as I have had to make changes, sorry."

Kev and Sully made their way to the photography edit suite within the department.

"Sully, I'm going to show you what I do, but if I don't make anything clear please stop me and we'll go over it again. The first thing we do is check the Coroner's open case folder."

Kev tapped on the keyboard, entering his username and password. The screen displayed multiple folders all arranged in different areas on the screen. He double-clicked the mouse over the top of a folder titled "Coroner's Open." The screen instantly changed to display a long column of thumbnail folders, each of which had a Coroner's Number below it. "So as you can see, Sully, four of these have a red text title, that tells me the photos in them have not been edited yet. This bit is particularly important: any of the red titled folders must be copied now."

Kev highlighted the files, copied them, and placed them in a new folder titled Edited Case Photos. Then he changed the text colour of the original folders to black. If the Doctors need to show a court any photos we have taken they must not have been edited in any way. Kev then opened one of the folders and showed Sully what he could do with the editing tools.

"So, what is the point of doing any editing?", Sully enquired.

"Well, the doctors do presentations to junior doctors or their counterparts, so I clean up the images for that type of presentation. Have a go, Sully." Sully swapped chairs with Kev and soon got the hang of most of the editing program tools.

Later in the morning, Peter gave Suzie a call, "Hi Suzie, it's Peter. How are you all doing?"

"Very well. We're just about to go in and see him."

"How is he?"

"Still very sore but he will be fine. Hey, I was going to call you earlier, but Mum and I went for a walk along this amazing beach, and I didn't take my phone. Anyway, yesterday afternoon on the way here we ordered chocolates for you all. Did you receive them?"

"Yes, we did, thank you. But if any of the team get sick, I'm going to arrest you for the crime." They both laughed.

"Peter, when I get home in a few days can we go out together?"

"Of course we can. That would be lovely."

"Yes it would."

They chatted for a couple more minutes before Peter had to attend a meeting.

"See you later then Peter. Take care. I love you."

"Love you too. Bye."

After Sully had been editing for a couple of hours, he and Kev decided to go for lunch. Instead of playing chess with the others, Kev went out for a walk around the park on the other side of the car park, pausing every now and again to listen to the birds and admire the shape of the trees. He got his notebook and pen out of his pocket and jotted down notes as the thoughts came into his head, ' *I wonder if that could work?,* he thought to himself, ' *I'll have to sit down with the laptop tonight for a couple of hours and see if these ideas fit.'* Then his mind wandered about the conversation he'd had with Darren. Sitting himself down on a bench, he pondered the idea of being the new manager for the Mortuary.

CHAPTER FOURTEEN

FRIDAY

KEV WOKE EARLY FROM a disturbed night's sleep. On the way to the toilet, he flicked the switch to turn on the kettle. After washing his hands, and waiting for the kettle to finish boiling he made himself a coffee and added just a splash of milk to the cup. Holding the cup in his left hand and picking up his lighter and a cigarette in his right hand he went outside. Sitting on a chair he lit the cigarette; Kev glanced over to the model of the lighthouse by the back door and winked at it. Then, lighting the cigarette he thought to himself. ' *Yes I know today. It has to be, today.'* Sent in and approved today.

Peter was talking to Robert at Robert's desk; all the others had arrived for the morning briefing in the incident room. He finished the conversation with Robert then made his way to the whiteboards to the side of the room. He reached halfway up one of the boards and tapped his fingers five times; the room fell silent.

"Morning everyone. Today's the day, I can feel it. Day ten already! Fe, the Super's PA, has informed me the Super is getting twitchy with the amount of his budget we're going through, so we need this wrapped up today. Basically, we think that this has all been connected to a treasure hunt, and we think it must have been Sam who found the clue that Eric found in the lighthouse. To stop Sam running off to find the hoard on his own, he was killed. If the other three that we know of, followed Sam into the lighthouse and saw the same clue, then tonight being the first full moon, I'm sure things are going to take a big step forward. We have nothing on Pomeroy so far, other than the connection with the missing coins. If we can, let's nick the other two on a charge of breaking and entering for starters, but getting them in here is key. When we question them, I think we may get them to tell us everything. With all that in mind, I want someone to be watching the feed from the cameras. If we see Pomeroy or the other two anywhere around the harbour or the light, then I want to know instantly. Shani, can you organise that, please?"

"Yes Sir, I will."

"Ken, you take the rest of the day off – and please stay away from the pub before you meet up with the police and rescue boat crews tonight."

"Yes Sir, I will. Also, the coxswain of the rescue boat has already called me this morning. He says the weather conditions for tonight are supposedly going to be perfect."

"Good, good. Nikki, you're taking Mrs Heartland to the airport today, yes?"

"Yes, Sir."

"Please pass on our condolences and thank her for the information she gave us. Wish her a safe trip back to London."

"Will do, Sir."

"Anna, as soon as we get our eyes on Pomeroy, track all his movements with the CCTV cameras. If we get a case against him, I need it to be solid."

"Sir."

"Okay, let's get on."

Kev was sitting in the large armchair in the corner of the tea room, reading the paper. He had already changed into his scrubs and was just whiling away some time before the others arrived for the morning meeting. His phone pinged. He took the phone out of his pocket, removed his glasses, and opened the text message. *Thank you for your submission earlier today. We will process it immediately. Please could you make yourself available for a team's meeting with Mr Sandy at nine a.m. this coming Saturday, your time. Regards Kathy, personal assistant to Mr Sandy of Books and Co, U.S.A.*

At the morning meeting a short while later, Darren said.

"I'm covering your on-call tonight aren't I, Kev?"

"Yes, if that's still okay? I was going to ask you if you could cover until ten in the morning. I have something I need to do at nine and don't want to be in the middle of a call out."

"That's fine. I'll leave you a note about anything that happens so you can see it if you come in. Mike can you review everyone's training records and make sure we are all up to date, thank you. Bianca You are with Malloy today and Alison can you show Sully how you remove the femur and the pacemaker of Doctor Peters patient when he is ready for them. Joe please clean the fridge room and the trolleys please. Kev, can I see you for a second in my office? Thankyou everyone"

When they were inside the office, Darren closed the door, and said, "I know we have a few hours left but I was wondering if you had had a chance to consider what we were talking about the other day?"

"Yes I have Darren, and here's the thing, I have decided I do not want the job."

"Oh Kev, sorry to hear that. Well, I hope you support Alison as much as you have me. She will be offered the position and I am quite sure she will accept it judging from conversations I have had with her regarding her career path. I am sure the next manager, Alison, or someone else will appreciate your support as much as I have. Thankyou Kev. I am sorry for you making that decision but I know you know your limitations and what you have to do to be able to get by day to day without feeling inadequate I will inform them this afternoon."

Peter called Suzie, "Hi, how are you this morning?" "Good morning, Peter, I'm very well, thank you. Paul is still in pain, but they are going to discharge him today, and they want to see him twice a week. Dad has found us a house that we can rent. Mum doesn't want any other doctors seeing Paul, so she wants to stay close by."

"How long do you think you'll stay?"

"Well, Dad has rented the house for a month."

"A month? Well, if I get this case closed, maybe I can come up for a long weekend."

"Yes, please do. I miss you."

"I miss you , as well." Looking up, he saw the Superintendent standing in his doorway, "Take care. I have to go; I'll call back later." "Morning Sir," he said to the Superintendent.

"Sorry, Peter, I didn't mean to disturb your call."

"No, that's fine. I was just checking on Paul's condition."

"Is he going to pull through?"

"Yes Sir, he will. The doctors have said that they will discharge him from hospital later today."

"Oh good, good. Now, the reason I am here. Can you run through your plan for tonight with me?"

"Yes, Sir. Please take a seat."

Kev was mopping the corridor that ran the length of the department alongside the doors to the fridge bays helping Joe out, when Darren called out.

"Kev, I'm just off to the meeting. Are you sure of your decision?"

"Yes Darren, I am sure. See you later. And thanks again for covering tonight."

"No worries. Take care. Bye for now."

Just then, the automatic internal door to the autopsy room swung open. Bianca was standing in the doorway.

"Hey Kev, I've got a visitor for you."

Kev looked up and saw Liz coming through the door. "Cheers, Bianca! Stay there, Liz. I'll come to you – the floor's wet."

"Hi, I was going to leave you a note but when Bianca saw me, she told me to come through. Is that all right?"

"Of course. It's good to see you."

"I was just going to ask if you were still okay to go out tonight? I was thinking about six if that suits you. Mum will have had her dinner by then."

"Yes, that's fine. I'm looking forward to seeing your mum again."

"And what about me?"

"Yes, and you. I won't hug you as I am a bit dirty."

"No worries. See you later." She leant in towards him and they kissed.

Kev got home just after five. He had already showered before leaving work, so all he had to do before going to see Liz was iron a couple of shirts. After storing the iron and the board, he kicked off his shoes and headed for his bedroom. He took out a pair of pre-ironed dark blue jeans, went to the bathroom, applied some more deodorant, and headed back downstairs. He drank a glass of water before putting on the jeans and shirt. He drew the curtains and turned on the hall light as it would be dark by the time he came home. Then he picked up a small thin plastic box from the kitchen table, placed it in his front pocket, and left. He locked the door and started walking to Liz's mum's house.

When he arrived twenty-five minutes later he checked his watch before ringing the doorbell. Five past six. Liz opened the door and launched herself into his arms.

"Hello, you!" She gave him a long kiss, her hands cupping his bottom, then stood back and looked Kev up and down. "I love those jeans on you – they make your little bum nice and round." She turned as she said that and held her hand out behind her. Kev took hold of it and she led him into the house.

"Thank you." Liz turned her head a little to smile at him as she opened the door to the lounge room before saying.

"Mum, Kev's here."

Betty turned down the volume on the program she was watching.

"Good evening Betty. Good to see you again."

"Good evening Kevin. How are you?"

"Better now, I've finished work for the day."

"Yes, Liz told me what you do for a living. Working in a Mortuary must be stressful."

"Yes, it can be. Luckily, we have a good team, and we all look after each other."

"Kev, come through to the kitchen. I'm just making Mum a cup of tea."

"Excuse me, Betty. I'll go and get your tea and I'll be back in a second."

Kev walked to the end of the lounge and looked round the open door. The first thing he saw was a round table with two typewriters on it. Moving forward, he looked round and saw that Liz was just stirring the tea.

"So, are these the typewriters you were talking about?"

"Yes, they are."

"Well, if you find me some paper, I'll take in your mum's tea and then I will have a look at them."

Liz went into the hallway and Kev took Betty's tea to her.

"There you go, Betty. Shall I put it down here?"

"Yes please. Thank you, Kevin."

"Betty, we're just in the kitchen. I will have a look at the typewriters for you."

Kev made his way back to the kitchen. Liz was just coming back down the hallway, holding out a few sheets of paper for him. Both typewriters were in the same condition, but one was slightly older than the other, not the sort that Kev would search for on Saturday mornings. He loaded a sheet of paper into the older one first and started typing away at the keys. After ten seconds or so, he loaded the other one with paper, and another few seconds went by with him tapping the keys. Then he took the plastic box from his pocket, put it on the table and opened it up, revealing a range of small-scale tools.

"Oh, Wow! They're cute, are you fixing them now?"

"Yes, if you like. It will only take me half an hour."

"Are you sure?"

"Yes. You go and sit with your mum, and I'll tell you when I'm done."

Liz kissed him on the cheek and left. Twenty minutes later, Kev called her to have a look. When she came in, she looked at the fresh pages on each of the typewriters. On the older one, Kev had typed on the page: "Both of us are in good working order now." On the other one, he had typed: "Can we please get food now? I am hungry xx."

Liz wrapped her arms around him and gave him a kiss, "Of course we can. Let's go and say goodbye to Mum. We're off now Mum. Kev has fixed your typewriters. Leave them in the kitchen and I'll take them back upstairs when I get home. I should be home before midnight, we are going to the Yacht Club for dinner. Call me if you need me." She bent down and kissed her mother goodbye.

"See you later, Betty. Take care."

"Yes, and thank you, Kevin, for doing that, fixing them. Take care. Be careful and come home safe."

"We will, Mum. See you later."

Liz took Kev's hand and they left.

CHAPTER FIFTEEN

IT TOOK KEN FORTY minutes to drive to the Inshore Rescue clubhouse from his home address. When he got out of the car, he was greeted by the two coxswains. Mark, from the police boat (which was at anchor about a hundred yards offshore) and George, the coxswain of the Inshore Rescue boat for that evening.

"Look at that water, Ken. Flat as a pancake George said."

Ken looked out. It really did look beautiful; silver tips of dancing water for as far as the eye could see. He felt as if he could just stretch out his arm and touch one of the biggest and brightest full moons he had ever seen that was causing these conditions. The moon that night had been mesmerising him all the way there.

"Beautiful isn't it," all three stood there for a few seconds. "Come on, let's get you kitted out."

Ken grabbed his bag from the boot of the car and followed the two men into the clubhouse. Three-quarters of an hour later, he was wearing items from the storeroom and looked the same as all the other crew members of the rescue boat. They had dressed him in a dry suit and an over suit belonging to an off duty crew member. Then they assisted him into one of the latest lifejackets and lastly George gave him a crash helmet.

"Right, Ken, follow me up these steps. We'll get into the rib now. Copy every step I take and then we will prepare to launch."

Before long, the four crew members and the extras (Ken and Mark) were safely on board. George sat in his position behind the wheel and turning to Ken said, "Ken mate, make sure you hold on to that strap and this handle here on the side of the console when we're on our way down the slipway. We hit the water at approximately thirty kilometres an hour, so it does give you a good jolt. Bend your knees a little before the impact and try to hold your breath on the way down, to stop your stomach doing a somersault. It can make you feel extremely sick. Are you ready?"

Ken nodded and George looked over both shoulders to make sure the rest of the crew, and Mark, were in position and ready. He pressed a button on the control panel in front of him. The two red and blue flashing light strips at the top of the roll-over bar (which also housed the self-righting air bags for the boat) lit up the boat house with a strobe effect, that dazzled Ken when he turned to see where the reflection on the wall was coming from. The rest of the ground crew lined the slipway to make sure no one got in the way of the craft as it made its way to the water. As it was dark, they held up glow sticks to indicate to the coxswain that the route was clear and ready for them to launch.

George turned on the ignition and made sure the engines were lowered to the almost vertical position. Vertical was the optimum position, for the engines to be in but positioning them like this made sure they wouldn't contact the trailer on the way down, to the water. He called out, "Prime!" and the two crew members standing on each side of the boat, behind Ken and Mark, bent down and squeezed the fuel pump pressure controllers until they went hard. Then they returned to their ready positions. The fourth crew member, who was standing directly behind George, called out, "Primed."

George took one last look over each shoulder then stood up to see if the ground crew were still in position with their glow sticks held aloft. If he saw just one stick at night, or one arm not held aloft during daylight, that would indicate that there was a problem, and they should not launch. Content with seeing all glow sticks raised, George sat back down and shouted out, "Launch!" On the ground level behind the boat, one of the ground crew knocked a steel pin out with a short-handled sledgehammer, to release the two cables attached to the back of the trailer. The trailer instantly began to slide down the slipway on its rails. Ken's breathing became audible to the others as his heart rate increased. His knuckles were white from the amount of force he was using to hold on to the handle and strap as the trailer picked up speed.

George pushed a button on the console and the two five hundred-horsepower outboard engines fired into life, making Ken jump. By this time, he could only breathe through his gaping mouth. He could see that they were just about to hit the water and remembered to bend his knees slightly. He was glad he did. When they hit, it still jarred his back a little, but it would have been worse if he hadn't remembered in time for the impact. He did, however, forget to hold his breath, and his stomach did turn over.

As soon as they hit the water and the boat had floated off the submerged trailer, the crew members quickly released two ropes that attached the boat to the trailer, and George lowered the engines the rest of the way. The fourth crew member, standing directly behind George, shouted out, "Released!"

George pushed the throttle forward and the craft took off at an amazing speed across the top of the almost waveless water. He steered the craft in a very wide circle around the police boat and came to a stop next to it. A couple of ropes were exchanged between the boats' crews, and after patting George on the back, Mark made his way carefully onto his boat.

A couple of minutes went by as Mark made sure his craft was ready. As soon as the crew of the police boat saw the navigation lights come on, they set about releasing the ropes that held the two boats together. The anchor chain rattled away at the bow of the police boat as the chain motor lifted the anchor. As soon as Mark saw on his console that it was up and locked in place, he gave George a thumbs-up and the two captains pushed their throttles forward to half speed. The boats' bows lifted effortlessly out of the water and they set off along the coastline, travelling about a hundred yards apart so neither would be affected by the other's wake.

At that point, Ken noticed his phone had lit up inside the waterproof pocket on his life jacket. Holding on with his left hand, he removed it from the pocket and tapped the screen. The camera app lit up, he tapped the screen again, and saw an image of Pomeroy's face. The message below the image said:

"Camera one activated".

Ken leaned in close to George, "How long until we get to the cave?" he asked.

"At this rate half an hour, but we can go faster."

"Do it full speed but when we get there, we need to be absolutely silent."

"Roger that! I'll let Mark know our intentions."

At that moment, Ken's phone vibrated. He looked, tapped on the app again and was shown an image of a boat entering the cave, with two men on-board. He was sure they were the two wanted for the break-in on *Seabreeze*. Ken quickly phoned Peter.

"Sir it's Ken. Get everyone to the lighthouse! Pomeroy is in the tunnel, and we have the other two in the cave, in a boat."

"On our way Ken. And Ken, silent approach. See you soon."

Ken tapped George on the shoulder and nodded. George picked up the radio handset, pushed the button and said, "Whisky One, Whisky One, do you receive? Over. This is Rescue One come in. Over."

"Whisky One to Rescue One. Received, over."

"Full speed but silent approach, over."

"Received, over."

Both boats' bows lifted a little higher, then the boats flattened out as the engines reached maximum speed. The craft had sped up so quickly Ken almost lost his phone over the side. He managed to secure it back in the pocket before he had to hang on again with both hands.

Peter made the call to get all available police units to the lighthouse, stressing that a silent approach was needed. He then ran out to his car and sped off towards the lighthouse, leaving tyre marks on the tarmac.

Just around the headland from the cave, the rescue craft was just in front of the police boat when George raised his hand and cut the throttle. Both boats came to a virtual stop at the same time, but were then rocked up and down and from side to side a few times as their wake swirled the water around and under them. In the police boat, Mark took the lead, with just enough throttle, to keep them moving forward. The rescue boat held back a little but then followed them using only the idle speed from the engines.

A brief time later, the radio crackled into life. "Whisky One to Rescue One. Come in, over."

"Rescue One to Whisky One. Receiving, over."

George listened intently to the information he was receiving through his earpieces. He removed one of the earpieces and turned to Ken, "They're using an infra-red camera to record what they can see," he said, "and are sure they have not been observed. They have one man by the tunnel, and he's just passed something to the two men in the boat. How do you want them to proceed?"

Without hesitation, Ken made the decision that these were the people they were after, "Tell them to get in there now and arrest all three."

"Rescue One to Whisky One. Arrest them! I repeat, proceed to arrest." Without any further communication from Mark to George, the police boat lit up like a Christmas tree and the massive engine roared into life. Within seconds, the police boat was blocking the entrance to the cave and two huge spotlights, mounted on top of the cabin, were turned on and positioned onto the subjects. One was pointed at the boat with two occupants in front of them, and the other was pointed onto the person by the tunnel.

Mark then used a mike on his console to project his voice into the cave, "This is the police! You are under arrest. Do not try to escape. We are about to board your craft."

The officers on board saw Pomeroy turn and run back into the tunnel. The small fishing boat had drifted away from the edge, and the two on-board were standing in the back with their hands up. As the police boat slowly moved closer to them, the police crew positioned themselves at the bow, waiting to see which side of their boat would end up next to the smaller craft. Mark checked the instruments to determine the best way to approach them, keeping a close eye on the depth which was fine in the middle of the cave but to this side there was shallow areas, he didn't want to ground the boat.

One of the officers at the bow of the police boat called out, "Prepare to be boarded! You are under arrest for an initial charge of breaking and entering." He noticed that the taller of the two men was holding a small hessian bag. At that point, the other man shouted, "You're a bloody idiot Jones! Why did you get me into this? First you kill those blokes and now this."

The police officers then saw the smaller man take a swing at the other. He hit him with such force that the man holding the bag went over the side of their boat. By the time the police had their boat securely tied up alongside, an officer had already dived into the water to rescue the unconscious man. When they had been helped back onto the police boat, Mark asked the officer.

"Did you get the bag he was holding before going in?"

"No, sorry Sir. I saw it fall out of his hand as he hit the water."

George had positioned the rescue boat in such a way that Ken was able to observe everything that unfolded.

At the lighthouse end of the tunnel, Peter arrested Pomeroy. He had started to run as he exited the tunnel, thinking he was in the clear. That's when five sets of car headlights suddenly illuminated the area. Peter ran after him and tackled him to the ground. Then he slapped a pair of handcuffs on him and informed him he was under arrest on suspicion of handling stolen goods, and being an accessory to murder. He and another officer led Pomeroy away to one of the waiting patrol cars.

When they got all three arrested men back to the Police Station, Peter decided to interview the smaller man from the boat first. Dominic quickly told Peter everything they had done, including that Jones had hit Sam with a hammer and got rid of it in the water, near to where they'd dumped Paul's body a few days later. Dominic was relieved to find out that Paul was alive and well, but that did not lessen his charges. One count of accessory to murder, breaking and entering and handling stolen goods. Pomeroy at his interview admitted that they had found the coins and their plan had been to smuggle them overseas. Jones and Dominic were going to be his go-betweens, his charges were accessory to murder, and handling stolen goods.

When Peter interviewed Jones, the left-handed person, didn't say a word during his interview; but with the evidence given by the other two, he was still charged with the murder of Sam and attempted murder of Paul; breaking and entering, and handling stolen goods.

Later the next morning, after Peter had had a couple of hours' sleep sitting in his office chair, he walked into the incident room and everyone stood up and started clapping.

"Thank you, everyone, thank you. Well done, Ken for getting there just at the right time."

Everyone faced Ken and continued clapping. Ken took a few bows and nodded around the room, acknowledging certain people for their help.

"And the biggest thank you everyone to, Eric. Without him finding that clue when he did, they may have got away with it all." They all continued to clap in Eric's direction. "Okay, settle down now. Let's get this written up. It's over to the courts now. Well done, all of you! All we need now is for the divers to find the coins at the bottom of the water in the cave, and I need to organise a search of the beach where Paul was found. Hopefully, we can recover the hammer, and then we can rest easy."

Meanwhile at Kev's house he was waiting for Mr Sandy's call. He had spent the time cleaning and doing some washing. He had his laptop open on the kitchen table, and to be honest, he was feeling a little nervous. When the chiming noise came from the computer, it made him jump. He took in a deep breath, exhaled and sat down in front of the screen and pressed the button.

"Hi, Mr Sandy. How are you?"

"Kev, my good friend," he replied. "Thank you for taking my call all the way from the Americas. This technology is brilliant, is it not? Listen, I would like to invite you to be the keynote speaker for our up-and-coming investors' tour. It will involve travelling to a few countries around the world, where we have investors. We will pay, of course. Flights, accommodation, food, and of course for your time. And all first class travel, I might add. As our newest author, we would like you to head it up. Oh, and by the way, before I forget, I have just authorised a payment to you of fifty-five thousand Australian dollars, from pre-ordered sales. Is that great or what? Hey, tell me why you put your own name to the mortuary technician character. Very macabre. I mean very, very macabre. But somehow, it works. We love it, we absolutely love it! Most authors put their name to a hero or top-ranking officer. Tell me how you thought up the story, *Murder at the Linley Cove Lighthouse?* I always like to know."

After a twenty-minute conversation, Kev closed the computer and picked up the first proof edition of his book. He had been sent it a couple of days before and the approval was the last submission he had made to the publisher.

"Well, my friend," he said aloud, looking at the book in his hand. "It looks like we are going around the world. I'd better ask for some time off – and tell everyone I have written a book, it's been published, and already selling fast."

ABOUT THE AUTHOR

Kevin is the third son of Robert George Hillier and Dorothy Margaret Hillier. Stephen and Andrew being his two older brothers. Kev was born in the lounge room of the family home soon after ten pm on the 21st of October 1966. His childhood was a good and loving one. From the age of fourteen, Kev worked in a butcher's shop after school. It was situated in the small village of Alverstoke in Gosport, Hampshire, on the south coast of England, to the left of Portsmouth Harbour.

When he left school, he gained a position with a large supermarket chain, working in their meat preparation room. That was, until he damaged an eye in an accident at home, which made it impossible to work with all the equipment at that time. After working in a few different departments over the next six months or so, he decided he needed something new.

He then worked for a maritime engineer, helping with everything from building or repairing slipways, to painting and varnishing yachts. At this time, Kev lived on a boat to try to save money, and that is when he started writing as he had no television. He would while away the hours in the evenings drafting stories that came into his head like waking dreams. These stories were handwritten in a book and wouldn't have been able to be read by anyone other than Kev due to his dyslexia. The stories were badly written, spelt and had hardly any punctuation.

After six months of working with the marine engineer, he joined a jewellery retail company as a trainee manager and made it to the position of manager a couple of years later. When a competitor bought out the company, Kev went for another change and became a trainee mortuary technician.

That's where he met Liz, you may say the rest is history. He is now settled in South Australia with Elizabeth and their two grown up daughters. He started writing again as a hobby in January 2023. After his father heard Kev had completed his first draft he said about the story "that should be published." Kev's father died three days later. Kev decided to approach a publisher and this is his novel. Thank you for reading it.

Milton Keynes UK
Ingram Content Group UK Ltd.
UKHW010643290124
436892UK00001B/26